Jade's Song

South of the Border 2

SABRINA DEVONSHIRE

To Madeleine,

Enjoy the escape!

Jade's Song
South of the Border 2

Published by Corazon del Oro
Communications, LLC
Cover Art by Anya Kelleye
ISBN-13: 978-1730970511

CHAPTER ONE

Jade

Brandon and I sit across from each other at a table in my favorite restaurant. It's a fancy Italian place in the Tucson Foothills. We've been together for eight years and finally, it's going to happen. I've waited for this day for so long. The day he asks me to marry him. I just know he's going to pop the question. I can just feel it. I'm jumping-out-of-my skin excited.

Brandon is good looking, has a great sense of humor, and a successful career as an investment broker. What woman wouldn't be happy to marry him? I mean, okay, things between us aren't perfect. He works late a lot and I spend a lot of nights alone on my computer. But whenever I ask him why he has to work until 2 AM, he kisses away my questions until I forget all about them.

Sure I was bummed that he cancelled a trip to La Jolla at the last minute. He had to stay on top of an important new client, he'd said. It was one of many disappointments. But this is what his job demands, and I'll get used to it. Like everyone else in corporate America, he has to work overtime to get ahead.

Now we're sipping Chardonnay and I'm wondering why he didn't order champagne. That's how this scenario is supposed to go. The champagne, the little black velvet box. Brandon on bended knee asking me to marry him.

Brandon clears his throat, and for a second glances away from me before meeting my gaze. "This isn't going to be easy. But I figured this would be the best way."

A wave of panic rolls over me. Something's wrong with this picture. Really, really wrong. He's not down on his knees. And he's not speaking to me like I'm the love of his life.

"I don't understand–"

"Jade, I don't want to hurt you. But our relationship isn't working out."

My throat feels like it's coated with sandpaper. My ears ring, and the room starts to sway. Oh, God, no. This can't be happening. I want to say something, but I can't. My jaw has locked up, frozen.

"I met someone else. She's right for me, Jade. You and I—we were never quite right for each other. You must have sensed that."

Did I? Then why was I expecting him to ask me to marry him? Did I conjure this all up in my mind—that he loved me? Or did he somehow fool me into believing it until it was convenient for him to tell me it was over?

"Jade, aren't you going to say anything?"

I look at the man across from me—this blond-haired, blue-eyed man I shared a bed with, shared hundreds of meals with, made love to so many times. And I realize he has become a stranger. That I never really knew him.

How could I have misjudged things—and him—so badly? His jaw's clenched and his brows are drawn inward. He's actually irritated with me. Because I'm not answering. I'm not telling him it's fine that he wants someone else.

What does he expect? For me to look him in the eye and say, "Sure, no problem. I don't mind that you are discarding me like yesterday's leftovers." Or maybe that's why he brought me here in the first place—because he knew I'd be super upset and figured if we were in public, I wouldn't make a scene.

Well he's in for a surprise. "Yeah, I am going to say something." I rise from my seat. "I'm leaving." I drop my cloth napkin on the table. I don't want to remember the birthdays and holidays when we sat at this same table. All I want to do is get the hell out of this place.

"Wait, Jade. We're not finished talking. We haven't had dinner yet."

"I'm not hungry. For obvious reasons. I'll take an Uber back to my house."

"Let me drive you home at least. We can talk more then."

"It's not your home, it's my house. And you're no longer welcome there. I'll pack your stuff and leave it outside for you." Or maybe I'll throw it all in the back of my pickup truck, take it downtown, and give it to homeless people.

He jumps up from his seat and grabs my arm. "It doesn't have to be like this, Jade."

I twist away from his grip. "Don't put this on me. You made your choice. Now I'm making mine." Tears well up in my eyes. I bite my lip to keep them from spilling down my cheeks and speed past curious diners that have been watching the whole scene unfold. I can keep it together for a few moments. I clench my jaw and stride from the room, leaving my bleeding heart behind.

CHAPTER TWO

Jade

Facebook is my new best friend. Instead of meeting my daily writing word count, I now spend most of my days and nights lurking online, skimming other people's posts.

I click through photos taken in the south of France, another person's Switzerland hiking vacation, a photo of a cute fluffy dog that died. I select the sad face icon for the last post and write a short phrase of condolence. Then I browse through more vacation photos—of beaches in

Costa Rica, Mexico, the South Pacific. Bikini-clad women stand in shallow clear sea water smiling, sipping tropical drinks or holding a mask and snorkel. The locales pique my interest mostly because they're far away from here—the one place on Earth where I really don't want to be right now. In Tucson. Near Brandon. As hard as I try, I can't seem to wipe the man from my mind for even a minute.

What if scenarios break into my thoughts during the day and keep me awake late into the night. I keep wondering what made him change his mind about me. I keep thinking if I did this or that differently, he might not have hooked up with someone else and we might still be together.

I know he didn't want me to quit my engineering job to write full-time. Maybe that made him decide to end it. Or maybe he lost interest and started noticing other women because I dressed too sloppy around the house. Maybe if I'd worn more makeup or sexier clothes or—oh, damn—why do I keep torturing myself like this? If he didn't want me the way I am, I shouldn't want him anyway. I let out a frustrated sigh. If only it were that easy.

I glance at a list of suggested groups that pops up. Beach Vacation Homes and Condos. Expats Living in Mexico. Andes Mountain Tours. Wait, Expats Living in Mexico? That sounds interesting. No, it sounds outstanding.

That's something I could go for right now—running away to live in another country. I walk into the kitchen, pour myself a third glass of wine, and return to my computer. I click the link, then click again on the *Join* button. Minutes later, I've been added to the group and am reading strangers' posts.

One thread's all about Mexican towns and cities where people have relocated including all the pros and cons. Another's about how Americans can obtain permanent residency. There's another discussion about food—how you go about sanitizing fruits and vegetables, what kind of water filters to buy, where people should buy their meat, cooking with *nopal,* which turns out to be diced prickly pear cactus. Who knew you could make a meal with that? I wonder how you get the spines out.

And then there's talk about housing and how much people pay for homes and condos. My eyes widen when I see the numbers. Wow. Whether you rent or buy, it's dirt cheap to get a place compared to what we pay in the US.

I bounce in my seat with excitement. I could do this. Why the hell not? It would be great to escape and pretend this shit with Brandon never happened. I'd be so busy adjusting to the lifestyle differences, I'd stop thinking about how I just wasted eight years of my life with him. I could live on a beach somewhere. In Mexico, it would be affordable. Some of these homes and condos people are buying—in Mazatlán and Colima and Puerto Vallarta—cost way less than the house I own now.

The next week passes in a blur. I cull through my stuff and put my house on the market. My house sells in two days. The buyer wants to close in thirty days. Now what? I still haven't picked a destination. Mexico is a big country. And there are so many cool places to choose from.

After a marathon online research session, I pick San Carlos, near Guaymas, in Sonora, Mexico, for its beautiful beaches and the fact that it's only a seven-hour drive from Tucson. It's a safe gamble, I tell myself.

It's close enough to the States that I can easily come back if this crazy idea of mine turns out to be a mistake. But staring at photos of the deep blue Sea of Cortez and all the offshore islands makes me think it could never be anything short of amazing.

My skin prickles with excitement. I play an electronic dance music mix on my iPad. I snap my fingers and sway my hips to the beat as I pack my suitcases. I love this plan. I can't wait to leave here, to go somewhere new where I have no bad memories to weigh me down. For years, I've wanted to travel. Brandon and I took a few trips, but we never went anywhere unusual.

I told Brandon I'd always wanted visit Costa Rica or Greece, but he said there were dangerous pythons and huge spiders in Costa Rica and that Greece was a poor country full of desperate people. So we vacationed in Florida, which was nice, but not the least bit exotic.

I wanted to see toucans and brightly colored scarlet macaws in Costa Rica and swim in the blue Aegean Sea off the coast of Greece. All these urges have nudged me in the ribs for years. Now,

I can finally give in to them. I no longer have to worry about what Brandon wants—what any man wants. I'm free. I can do whatever I want. And right now, I want to move to Mexico.

I shouldn't have told my sister I was leaving. But I figured someone related to me should know, and she's kind of it as far as family goes. Kelsi said moving to Mexico was the stupidest idea I'd ever come up with, almost as dumb as quitting my job to become a full-time writer. "Everyone sells drugs down there," she said. I rolled my eyes and shook my head at that. Like no one's selling drugs in Tucson.

But that conversation's long over. I'm ready to run. Away from that limiting logic that says I have no other choice other than to stay here and wallow in my misery and spend half the day tied up in traffic jams.

Tucson has never been right for me. Since Brandon dumped me, it's become more apparent than ever. The barrenness of the place and all the chaos of traffic and constant construction depresses me. It makes me feel lost—like I can't keep up with a pace I have no desire to keep up with.

Every day, I seek solace in the pool. Underwater, it's quiet. During that hour I swim from end to end, the anxious chatter in my mind slows down at least temporarily. But it returns the minute I climb out of the pool. This week when I swam, I heard the water rush past my ears and imagined I was swimming in the Sea of Cortez. Floating over a wave, smelling the salt in the air and gazing up at the sky. Maybe in the sea, I can finally find freedom, instead of remaining a prisoner of my own negative thoughts.

CHAPTER THREE

Jade

Arizona disappears in my rear-view mirror as I cross into Mexico. After following cars in front of me through a maze of barricades and braking several times for large speed bumps, I am officially across the border. On the opposite side of the road, where cars are approaching the U.S. border, Mexican soldiers wearing camouflage uniforms patrol the road with semi-automatic rifles. The machine guns I've seen before are in movies. Seeing them just feet away is unnerving.

The road narrows to a corridor walled by unstable cliffs of rock on one side and chain-linked fence on the other. I drive on, catching glimpses of Nogales—the Sonora side—as I go. Randomly oriented, cement block houses obscure most of the arid hillsides.

A red-rimmed triangular sign with a black image of boulders tumbling down a cliff warns drivers about falling rocks. I don't need to see it to know rocks are a threat here. Orange and white rocks litter the road and the shoulder.

I see a black and white pickup truck with flashing lights driving in the opposite direction. *Policía Federal* it says on the side of the truck. Did I do something wrong? I watch the truck get smaller and smaller in my rear-view mirror. I release a long exhale. Maybe here the police always drive with their flashing lights on?

That's something no one ever mentioned on the Facebook pages. I wipe away sweat from my forehead. I've never even driven in another country before. Everything looks so alien, so unfamiliar.

Calm down, I tell myself. You'll get used to it after a while. I know I'm supposed to stop at a place 21 kilometers beyond the border to get my papers stamped. I already applied for permanent residency at the Mexican consulate in Tucson.

I'll take some forms and my temporary visa to an immigration office near where I'm going, and in a month or so, fingers crossed, I'll be a resident. I approach an immigration checkpoint. There are lanes for trucks and autos, and another for vehicles with something to declare. I drive into a lane with a green *X* over it.

As I enter the narrow lane, a machine snaps a photo of me. When I get to the end and the gate bar pops up, I pull into one of the open lanes. Two young women in blue uniforms are drinking coffee and laughing. They don't look like they want to cause anyone any trouble.

So why am I so nervous? All I have to do is use my limited Spanish to tell them what's in my car and they should let me pass unmolested. Hopefully. I lower the window and say, *Buenos Días*. One of the women glances away from her companions, masks a yawn with one hand, and leans toward my window. After returning my greeting, she asks in Spanish, *What's in your car*?

My suitcases with clothes, books, and sports equipment, I manage to stammer out in Spanish. I don't mention my laptop or smartphone. It says online I can bring those into the country without paying duty, but I'm worried if I say too much, they'll want to open every suitcase and they will burst out laughing when my ten boxes of tampons fall out. But seriously…One has to be prepared, just in case. For all I know, they only sell jumbo maxi-pads down here.

I'm not in much of a mood to carry on a conversation. It's intimidating enough traveling to a strange country. Having to explain myself to strangers in Spanish when I'm already way out of my comfort zone feels like too much. I know my expectations are unrealistic. I wanted to run away from my life. I wanted adventure. But I wasn't prepared to face the scary unknowns of being in an unfamiliar country. I let out the breath I didn't realize I'd been holding when the woman waves her hand forward and says, *Adelante.*

Shortly after immigration I encounter a toll booth. The sign in front of it says *Prepare su cuota.* The amount due is displayed on a digital display, which makes the toll payment quick and easy. Soon, I'm back on my way. But then there's road construction. And it's a scary mess. I almost miss the turn off for kilometer 21.

I park the car, make a beeline to the bathroom for a stress-relieving pee and then enter the building where I'm supposed to get my visa and passport stamped. Several people stand ahead of me in line. The odor of bleached floors and sweaty bodies assaults my nostrils. The room is hot and stuffy. The temperature outside is already well over 90. It can't be much below that in here.

My shoulders slump forward as my muscles wilt from the heat. Finally, it's my turn. I mask a yawn as I greet the dark-skinned man with the green uniform behind the counter. Deep lines mar his forehead. Dark rings under his eyes suggest he either has one hell of a hangover or didn't sleep well. He asks me where I'm going.

I'm moving to San Carlos, I say in Spanish. I realize, too late, that my voice sounds too jubilant and innocent. Like I'm moving into a new dorm room or something. Maybe that's why the lines on his forehead multiply and now he has a unibrow. I bite my lip nervously, feeling idiotic.

The stamp in his hand pauses inches above my visa paper as he studies me and his lips purse in puzzlement. He's wearing that same doubtful expression I saw on the faces of everyone I told about this crazy plan of mine. He, like all of them, must think I'm a complete nutcase to be moving down here.

But it's not too late. I can make a U-turn, go back to the States, and tell everyone this was all a terrible mistake. The thump of the stamp on my visa and passport snaps me back to reality. The man pushes my documents in my direction, offers a faint smile, and tells me to enjoy my life in San Carlos. *Gracias*, I answer. As I walk back to my car, I tell myself I'm not going back to Tucson. I'm going to give this adventure a fair chance.

Back on the highway, I slam on the brakes when a construction vehicle veers in front of me without warning. When I saw the *Entrada y salida de camiones* (trucks entering and exiting) sign, I figured the drivers might at least look before veering onto the highway. Geez.

The highway alternates between a divided four-lane highway and a two-lane highway, with intermittent detours (*desviaciónes*) separating them. Often the orange signs that indicate a lane is disappearing are reversed, so when I think the right lane is ending, it turns out to be the left. The four-lane sections are similar to US highways.

But on those narrow stretches where semis barrel toward me and cars make dangerous passes, it's a nightmare. Beside the road, construction vehicles are digging and pushing earth, raising clouds of reddish-brown dust into the air.

I get trapped behind a slow-moving truck. The road is windy. Suspended dust swirls in the air. The view ahead is too obscured for me to make a safe pass. But that isn't a deterrent to everyone. Two cars veer around me, overtaking my car and the truck in front of me. One drops in ahead of the truck just before another line of oncoming cars appears. Talk about a near miss. This is insane. I'm never going to make it to San Carlos alive. Maybe I should just follow the truck. At least it will make a good buffer if some idiot on the other side attempts a suicide pass.

I lower the volume on the radio. This is no sing-along drive. It's more like a plead with God that I won't die today drive. The kamikaze passing continues. Bulldozers and tractors move earth just inches from the road. A large team of men operate a metal machine the width of two lanes that is spreading concrete to construct what will one day be the other side of the highway.

I drive through the town of Santa Ana. There are people on bicycles. Pedestrians—even whole families with young children—dart across the road. Cars and trucks swerve randomly out onto the highway. Do they even look to see if anyone's coming? And then there are the damn *topes*. The way high speed bumps that could bounce the teeth right out of your mouth if you miss seeing them. I brake for another *tope*. Even rolling over it slowly rattles my brain.

The locals use the slowing traffic as a sales opportunity. A skinny man wearing a shiny green and yellow soccer jersey holds up packages of freshly-made tortillas. A woman wearing a bright red blouse tucked into jeans so tight, she looks like she was poured into them waves bags of grapes toward me. I smile and shake my head. Another man runs up to my car, tapping on the glass to show me what looks like packages of spices. This feels so awkward. I can't even remain anonymous in my car driving.

I finally reach a stretch of four-lane road that lasts for more than five minutes. I breathe out a sigh of relief and turn up the volume on the radio. It's a Mexican station, so the songs are all in Spanish. But I've always liked Latin music. So much of the music is happy and has a great beat. American music has become so depressing lately. Turning on the radio to hear a whiney-voiced singer belt out, *I just want to die* doesn't do much to boost my morale when my boyfriend of eight effing years dumped me.

Melodies blur from one to another as I drive across a barren stretch of desert toward Hermosillo. All at once, a song pulls me out of my trance. The man's deep, sensual voice makes my speakers and my skin vibrate. What an incredible voice. I feel like I'm being seduced note by note. The rich sound of his baritone voice is so sexy and masculine, it makes my nipples tingle. I hear the words *amor* and *corazón*. He's singing about love.

A visual image of the mysterious singer pops into my mind. I see a tangle of dark hair, large expressive eyes, and thick, full lips. His deep and resonant singing voice suggests he's large and powerful. Maybe even an athlete. I imagine his biceps flexing as he holds the guitar in his lap while he sings. The mysterious man's eyes are closed, his brows drawn together as he immerses his senses in the passion and love he's feeling. A wave of jealousy rolls through me. I suddenly wish that his lyrics of love and longing had been written just for me.

As I tap out the rhythm on the steering wheel, I grasp to catch more of the lyrics. But I barely know Spanish. If I could just remember the lines of the refrain I might be able to search for the song and download it. This romantic Spanish ballad. With jazzy sounding instrumental accompaniment.

I wonder what genre they call this kind of music down here. This song moves me in so many ways. I want to listen to it over and over again and imagine that this mysterious man is in love with me. What can it hurt? He's not real, so having a silly crush on him is totally safe. Maybe the distraction of it and this change of scenery will be what I need to wipe Brandon from my mind for good.

The song ends. The loss of the singer's comforting voice is jarring. For a few minutes, I had felt as if he were here with me. The hollow emptiness in my chest that's been there since Brandon dumped me yawns larger than ever before. The end of the song reminds me that I'm completely alone in a strange country.

I'll arrive in San Carlos in a few hours. But there will be no lover waiting to pull me into a tight hug, no group of friends asking me to join them for dinner. It will just be me driving into town alone and checking into a hotel room and having no clue where to go for dinner. In this strange town—like so many nights in Tucson recently—I'll lie in bed awake under the cold sheets, missing a man who never really loved me.

All I have is a memory of a song and a fantasy about a man I don't even know to fill the empty void inside my heart. And my new vibrator—the one that got over 500 five- star reviews on Amazon—to meet my physical needs. I'll get by on solo orgasms and romantic fantasies. I'm not interested in anything more than that. No hookups. No cozy chats. No lingering over breakfast. I won't lay my heart on the chopping block again. It's been sliced and diced badly enough already, along with my self-esteem. *No más*.

I don't have the kind of looks that stop men in their tracks like my sister. I'm not a best-selling author—I don't make a six-figure income. But I love what I do and I'm a human being with real feelings. That's worth something, at least to me. I won't let another man make me feel like an object that can be used and discarded when I no longer serve a purpose.

It's all well and good to imagine that some man will love me just the way I am. But it's not reality. I so don't want to have to lose ten pounds, go back to the engineering job I hated, or wear heels I can't even walk a straight line in just to please a man. I want to just be me. I want to learn to be satisfied with that regardless of what other people think. Instead of making a choice that works for me—like my recent resignation from my day job to write—and then beating myself up over it for days after someone like Brandon or my sister criticizes me for my decision.

"Dream on, Jade," I mumble to myself. Will I ever be able to like myself again after what happened with Brandon? I don't know. It's been thirty-two days since that fateful dinner, but I still feel as wounded and vulnerable as I did the morning after it happened.

Outside my car windows, the sky is a pristine azure, untainted by dust from roadwork. And so dry. I can't see a single cloud. I drive for miles without seeing a building, only distant, rock-and-earth mountains and acres of farmland. Traffic is light. But the cars on the road are either zooming by me at well over 80 miles per hour or going ridiculously slow—like maybe 55. I have to be alert every second. I try to drive the speed limit—100 kilometers an hour—in case there are *policia* around. The last thing I need is a ticket or *multa*. I read on the Mexico Facebook forums that some of the cops ask for bribes instead of writing tickets. They demand a few hundred dollars when the tickets usually are less than 50 dollars. I'm not sure how I'll handle it if I get pulled over, so it's better to avoid getting stopped.

A sign ahead says Guaymas, 220 kilometers. Guaymas is the sister city to San Carlos. I must be near Hermosillo. It's the largest city in the state of Sonora and I have to drive through it to reach my destination. On the city's outskirts, there are gas stations, manufacturing plants, small shops, and even a fancy resort. Soon the road is clogged with traffic. It's hard to tell where my lane ends and the next one begins. Apparently, I'm not the only one having that problem, because cars are drifting all over the road without signaling. Horns honk, and I hear the squeal of more than one car slamming on its brakes. Sweat drips down my face. Will I be able to get through this city in one piece?

The traffic lights are strange. They flash green before they turn yellow and then red. At least there's more time to prepare for the light change. Not that anyone pays much attention to the signals. Often one or more cars run the lights. To say you have to be alert when driving down here is the understatement of the year.

My GPS indicates to make a left turn on the *Periférico*. Whatever that is. Maybe I'll be out of this mess soon. Near the intersection where I'm supposed to turn is a cement plant and some ugly, run-down buildings. Several large semis are in the line to turn as well.

I drum my fingers on the steering wheel, waiting for the light to change. Two young boys dash up to my car and pour dirty water on the windshield. Waving them away doesn't work.

They wipe and smear until I can barely see out the window.

Despite the disastrous cleaning job, they expect some payment. I power down the window a few inches and hand over some peso coins I got as change from the toll booths.

They run toward the next hapless victims in the car behind me. The cars and trucks ahead of me begin moving. There's no time to deal with my messy windshield. I follow the line of traffic around the corner and drive along a winding road. If I didn't have my GPS, I'd never know where to go. There are so many turns and stoplights and the lanes are narrow. I start to wonder if I would have been better off driving straight through *el centro*. At least I wouldn't be surrounded by all these trucks.

I drive alongside a yellow cement wall, adorned with colorful floral designs, toward an underpass, waiting to make a left turn. The lane

I'm in is narrower than ever. A truck pulls up beside me in the adjacent lane. It's only inches away. I grimace, waiting to hear the screeching sound of it peeling all the paint off the side of my car.

By some miracle, I make it around the corner unscathed. I pass an OXXO convenience store, another Pemex gas station, and the substations that supply the city's electricity. I turn on the wipers to clear away the mucky water from my windshield. I see only mountains and an endless stretch of highway ahead of me. I sigh with relief and wipe the nervous sweat from my brow. Finally, Hermosillo is behind me.

Now there's hope this drive is going to end soon. Fortunately, there's a long stretch of four-lane road with wide, cement lanes, plenty of shoulder and light traffic. Ninety minutes later, I take the San Carlos exit, wowed by the dramatic landscape. Jagged mountains of reddish-brown earth and rock are sparsely vegetated with cactus. Many are cone-shaped, like they were ancient volcanoes. The road into town is lined with palm trees. I catch a glimpse of a slice of cerulean blue ocean dotted with islands.

I drive past several tidy brick homes with wrought iron bars over the windows. A white building on a hill appears to be abandoned. I see more empty structures as I drive along.

Skeletons of construction projects that were never completed. There are no fancy digital billboards around here. Only old-style signs. There's a billboard about window coverings, a grocery store, and one encouraging visitors not to litter on the beach. Some flash bright colors and seem new. Others are tattered or are simply a cloth banner wrapped around a metal frame. San Carlos looks like a place that time forgot to take forward with it.

Where the road narrows, I catch my first expansive view of the Sea of Cortez. The brilliant blue-green color contrasts dramatically with the dry brown landscape. I'm overcome by emotion as I slow down to get a better view of this endless oasis.

A surge of pleasure bursts through the layer of sadness that's hung over me for more than a month. I practically squirm in my seat with excitement as I imagine immersing myself in that healing water. It was a good idea after all to come here. Every day I'll swim. And day by day, those swims will wash away my suffering.

The hotel where I'm staying has no beach—it's on the marina. But I see lots of beach parking as I drive along. I'll check in, then grab a few things, and head to the sea.

I pull up to the Marina Terra hotel and walk across the marble-floored lobby, once again noticing the heat. Don't they use air-conditioning in this country? My body feels heavy and exhausted and the dull throb on one side of my forehead telegraphs that a bad headache is about to strike. The front desk attendant greets me. I answer and show him my online reservation. Our voices echo in the high-ceilinged room. After only a few words of bad Spanish, the man begins speaking in clear, crisp English. I let out a sigh of relief.

Within minutes, I'm in my room. I don't bother to unpack. I slip on a swimsuit, grab a towel, my goggles and cap, and my key card.

Minutes later I'm where I want to be. Floating on my back, my body rises and falls with the motion of the salty blue-green waves. My breath slows until it synchronizes with the rhythm of the waves. I feel at one with these waves, which carry away my heavy thoughts, one my one until they are all gone and all that's left is sheer joy. The skin on my face tingles with elation. I watch pelicans glide over me. Clouds drifting across the sky. Time doesn't seem important anymore. The salty sea is supporting my body, embracing me. I feel so safe and serene, like I could stay out here forever.

Coming here was the best idea I've had in a long time.

CHAPTER FOUR

Jade

There's a real-estate office located in a strip mall just off the main boulevard. I ask the young woman at the front desk—who appears to be American—if anyone is available to show me properties. She says she will find someone and invites me to take a seat. A few minutes later, a balding man with sun-weathered skin approaches and greets me in English. "I'm Richard," he says, extending his hand.

We exchange small talk for a few minutes before getting down to business and discussing price range and what I'm looking for. I say I want to live by the sea. He says condos are my only option with the amount I have to spend. I say no problem. I'm not picky. Something simple would fit the lifestyle I want now anyway.

The first condominium complex Richard takes me to is right on the sea. He doesn't have a spec sheet with him, he says, but he can add me to a Mexican version of an MLS list where I'll be able to view all the details on this property and others he's planning to show me.

The white cement block buildings have cracked walls stained by streaks of rust from exposed rebar. We walk up a steep flight of stairs to the second-floor unit. Richard has to jiggle the key to get the door to open. The musty smell makes me sneeze the minute we step inside. The upholstery on the couch and chair is drab brown.

The life seems to have been beaten out of the cushions. They're misshapen and lumpy. The furniture comes with the place, Richard says, his voice pitching upward with enthusiasm. And that's supposed to be a plus? Doubt rushes in again. Can't I afford to buy something better than this?

I wander slowly around the small, two-bedroom apartment, trying to imagine myself living here. I'd need to live on Sudafed in this place. My sinuses are already congested, and I keep sneezing. I ask about the price. He says he thinks it's too high. I don't answer, but I'm thinking that's the understatement of the year.

"What else can you tell me about this property?" I walk outside on the balcony, waiting for Richard to follow me. The view of the blue-green water is mesmerizing. It looks so inviting, I want to leap off the balcony straight into the water. If I could overlook what's inside and sleep out on the patio every night, this place wouldn't be half bad.

"Most of the owners here rent their condos out so it's likely to be noisy. People coming from Hermosillo and Obregón like to party on the weekends. It's also vulnerable to hurricanes. The first floor of this complex has flooded more than once."

The place looks and sounds like a disaster. Why did he even bring me here? "This place isn't right for me at all. I can afford to pay more than you say this place is likely to be worth. Can you show me anything else?"

"Of course. I wanted to show you a less expensive place first, so you would have something to compare to what we're going to see next."

We leave the smelly condo behind and take the stairs to the parking lot. Richard turns toward me before getting into the car. "Now I'm going to take you to another condo complex on the beach called Bahía Delfin. It was built more recently. It's only ten years old."

I wait till I'm seated in the car before asking him another question. "What about hurricanes? Is that part of the beach very vulnerable, too?"

"The condos are well-built and set back further from the beach behind a seawall. No unit there has ever been severely damaged by hurricanes."

He backs out of the parking space and maneuvers onto the main road. He drives a couple of miles and then turns to the right. The road follows a huge estuary and leads to two condo complexes—one white, one terra cotta-colored.

We turn toward the earth-toned one. A security guard greets us at the gated entrance. Richard speaks to the guard in Spanish, shows identification, and only then does the guard raise the gate. It's nice that the place has security. After seeing so many wrought iron bars on home windows, I imagine break-ins must be a problem around here. The complex is large. Three-story buildings with red tile roofs sit in tidy rows on neatly manicured lawns. This place reminds me of upscale apartment complexes in the States.

Richard gives me a tour of the complex. I see amazing sea views, palm trees waving in the breeze, lush landscaping, and a lagoon-sized swimming pool, complete with lounge chairs, tables and a thatched roof palapa for shade. I know I should keep my game face on, but my excitement breaks loose. "This place is amazing," I burst out. Living here would be a dream. It's like a vacation resort.

"I'll show you a ground-floor unit first. The views won't be as good, but it will be easier for you to get your suitcases and groceries inside." He states the price.

It's within my budget. I clear my throat and try to speak in a calm voice. "I can work with that."

"You can get a lot for your money in Mexico right now. I think you'll like the floor plans, too."

The first two-bedroom condo is all white inside. Even the tile. It looks more like a hospital than a cozy living space. And there's not even a hint of Mexico in the place. "Hmm. I need some color. And some Mexican accents."

Richard sweeps his hand through the air. "There's an upstairs unit with Mexican tile in the kitchen and in both the bathrooms."

"I'd like to see that one."

"It's on the west side of the complex. You won't believe the views."

During the walk, Richard tells me about his move from Michigan to Mexico five years earlier. He moved to Mexico for health reasons—because the damp and cold winters up north aggravated his arthritis. Not only is his health better down here, he claims, but costs for healthcare are much more economical.

We ascend a steep staircase to a second-floor unit. Inside, the floors are Saltillo tile and the kitchen pops with bright yellow walls and countertops and backsplashes accented with colorful Talavera tile.

I smooth my hand across the cool glazed tiles. "What beautiful work." They have that handmade quality I've always been drawn to. Each tile looks like a work of art. Many of the shops in downtown Tucson sell mirrors and ceramics made in Mexico. All of them are hand-crafted and painted.

I never bought any of them because Brandon said they would detract from the sophisticated look of my place. At this moment, it feels good to realize that what Brandon wants no longer matters. I'm buying a place just for me. I want my home to burst with warmth, to be alive and full of vibrant color.

Two bedrooms are downstairs, and the Master bedroom is upstairs on the third floor. The first thing I do after I walk up the stairs is step out onto the balcony. My heart leaps in my chest. Wow. This is too amazing to believe. The view is… incredible. Like drone-view videos I see on the Internet. I can see an endless stretch of sea, rocky islands—two with flat tops and one with a "window" in the middle of the rock—plus the jagged, mountainous curve of the coastline, and most of the town of San Carlos from up here.

There's a wide stretch of beach, a stone wall, and two other condo buildings separating this building from the sea. Richard's right. The condo is set back enough so that it should be less vulnerable to hurricane damage. But it's still close enough to the water, I'd be able walk down to the beach and be swimming in the sea within minutes.

My stomach is turning somersaults. I'm so excited, I could jump out of my skin right now. I can't let Richard see how desperate I am to buy the place. I take a deep breath and feign calm and collected the instant I step back inside. He's talking to someone on his cell phone. I patiently wait for him to finish.

"What do you think?" he asks.

I nod and smile. "The unit is quite nice. Let's write up an offer."

CHAPTER FIVE

Jade

For two months now, I've lived in my dream condo by the sea. Every morning, I swim for an hour, sometimes longer. It's July and the water's warm, really warm—like barely cooled bathwater. During these long, hot, lazy days of summer, I swim just before the sun rises.

I wade into the shallow water, feeling the sand tickle my feet, and then plunge into the sea. Once I'm about 30 feet from shore, I swim parallel to the coast toward the El Soldado estuary. The sea wraps me in a warm embrace – it's so soothing, comforting. With my awareness of my movements and the sensation of water all around me, thoughts of Brandon slowly fade away and I start to feel whole again.

The sea is my only safe place. I know it's strange to say. Most people fear the ocean. They're afraid of sharks, stingrays, and jellyfish. But I feel at one with the natural world whenever I'm out here, immersed in the sea. My only worry is that that the time I have in the water won't be long enough. Because it feels so good – I wish I could stay out here forever.

Each exhale is a happy sigh as I propel myself over the waves. The salty water flows over my skin like massaging fingertips as I glide through the sea. I usually swim freestyle for long stretches, past the condominium complex where I live and the one beyond it until the shoreline I follow is just sand and mangroves. Less than a mile down the beach is the estuary. Herons, egrets, and even the occasional pink spoonbill make their homes in the swampy vegetation that encircles the large lagoon. I'm almost there now. Below me, I can see the sandy bottom, rippled by waves.

I breast stroke swim over a few dark volcanic rocks, which jut up from the sand and are overgrown with dark green seaweed and wispy pale pink sea fans.

Two puffer fish drift along below me. Schools of black-and-white-striped sergeant majors dart around and nibble on plants. In the shallow sea, small waves sigh over the sand. Seeking deeper water, I swim out further until I'm maybe a couple hundred feet from shore. The water's still shallow enough I could stand if I wanted to.

Submerging myself in the sea always makes me feel vibrant, alive. I stroke and kick my way along, relishing the sensation of the salt water sliding over my face, my back, my shoulders, my thighs. I swim faster. And faster. Adrenaline from the exertion jets through me. Happy chemicals dance in my brain. I flip over and swim backstroke. Wispy white clouds streak across the clear blue sky. Looking out to sea, the stretch of water looks endless. More than a hundred miles of sea separate me from the Baja Peninsula.

When I'm on my back, I have to trust that whatever's below me isn't in a biting mood. Or at least won't bite hard. I'm used to the nibbling fish—the shiny blue obelisks with yellow fins. They nibble on my feet, my inner thighs. And when I turn my head around and roar underwater at them, blowing bubbles and laughing, they dart away and then glide back to nibble on my vulnerable flesh the minute I turn away. Today we have been playing the scary face and nibble game most of the way to the mouth of the estuary.

That's where I find my dolphin friends. Five fins rise and then quickly dip beneath the surface. I don't understand them as well as I want to. I do know this is one of their favorite playgrounds. When I spot dolphins near the condos, they always seem to be on the move. On a mission. But down here they're always jumping and playing.

As I swim a slow breaststroke, I watch them leap and crash into the water. They have so much personality. Sometimes they are playful and childish. At other times, they appear purposeful and focused. Always, though, they are graceful and athletic. The way they arc and spiral through the water, they make swimming look effortless. A few flicks of their horizontally-oriented tail—the fluke—and they're rocketing through the water. The upstroke of the tail is preparation.

From careful observation, I know that their power comes from the downward thrust.

Two pods of dolphins frequent this bay. But I know this pod and they know me. Maybe they recognize me by my pink cap. Or the bright orange swim buoy I wear around my waist that tags along behind me for safety. Maybe without the cap, the buoy or the bright swim suit, humans all look the same to them. I'm only just learning to tell the dolphins apart.

Dolphins are so smart. I wonder what thoughts pass through their minds when they look at me. Do they ever wish they had hands to pick things up or write or build? Do they wonder why humans swim when we're so clumsy moving through the water compared to them? Do they worry about all the trash and other contaminants that humans have dumped into their living environment? Do they ever wish they could communicate with me, the way I always wish I could talk to them?

Fins rise and submerge. I glide along nearby, allowing them to decide whether to come closer. One dolphin dives and then surfaces, his dorsal fin visible just feet away from me. He's gray, with a white belly, like most of the members of this pod. In the direct sunlight, the dolphins appear almost black above water. Only underwater can you see their true colors. He arches over the water and dives again. I can see by the wake of water that he's approaching. My heart always beats faster when I know one of these magnificent creatures is beneath me. They're nine or ten feet long and probably weigh six hundred pounds compared to my five-foot four height and a hundred and thirty pounds of weight.

A dorsal fin knifes through the water just a foot or two away. When the dolphin dives again,

I duck my head underwater. The water's clear enough today that I can see his big body glide beneath me. So incredible. He moves so gracefully. Does he know I can see him underwater with my goggles on?

The dolphin plays a hide-and-seek game with me. I see a fin and then before I know it he's on the other side of me. Once he swims directly underneath me. All I can see below me is a huge gray shape with a long nose. People I see on the beach and out in the water on kayaks and paddleboards sometimes ask if I'm scared to be so close to these enormous creatures.

I always tell them how being near them isn't scary at all. I find being near the dolphins comforting. What about sharks and rays and eels? I usually shrug my shoulders because that's a complicated question to answer. And I figure my response wouldn't make any sense to a non-swimmer.

On land, there are bills to pay and appliances to fix and emails and calls to return. But swimming with the dolphins has this magical way of washing all my worries away. I belong out here in the sea. Here, I'm in my element, the stress of daily life forgotten. There is only this world of blue-green water, the gentle lift of the waves, gliding pelicans and squawking gulls. The appearance of another dark fin tells me more of my sea friends are approaching.

One dolphin zooms through the water, creating an enormous wake. He must be moving at more than twenty miles an hour. Other dolphins leap into the air and fall back down with a splash. I love to watch their tails. So wide and separated by two pointy fins.

Maybe I have tail envy. It would be amazing to be able to propel myself through this water at twenty miles an hour. I imagine how the water would feel sliding over the skin when moving that fast. I'd feel so sleek and powerful.

Another dolphin is behind me. I sense her before I turn around. Some of the dolphins have started to play rough, even slapping each other with their tails. The ones near me just glide slowly by. They sense somehow that they need to be careful around me. I hear clicking noises. And something else. A dolphin voice. Like a little squeak. Maybe I can understand them if we spend enough time together. One makes a particularly loud squeak and then glides away before I see the dolphin's fin moving toward shore.

I turn to watch the dolphin arc out of the water and dive down. And behind him, I see a wide stretch of beach. And one lone person. A man. He seems to be watching the dolphins through binoculars. He's fifty yards or more away, but I can see that he's hot.

Running shorts and a tight tank top showcase his lean, muscular physique. His messy dark curls have been tossed by the sea breeze. Another dolphin comes up beside me and then ducks underwater as if he's asking me to follow him. I glide behind him toward the shore while he bodysurfs the waves.

Most of the dolphins are frolicking in water less than three feet deep. They're rolling with the waves. Now the man I saw from far away is only a few yards away. What are these dolphins up to? If I didn't know better, I'd think they were trying to set me up with this guy. That's silly, but if they are, I can't fault their taste. This guy's a hot tamale if ever there was one. I can't tell if he's Mexican or American. But each feature I take in is more than a little distracting.

The aviator glasses he's wearing make him look like a total badass. His day-old beard accents the angular features of his face and the cute dimples that bracket full lips. Moving down to his body. Gulp. My mouth goes dry. My gaze wanders over every hard mound and ripple.

His tank top, damp with sweat, clings to his muscular torso. The man's got some serious biceps and triceps. They bunch and flex when he moves. His shoulders are broad and well defined. The sight of all that wet muscle in front of me makes my fingertips tingle. I imagine touching his amazing body. No. When another wave lifts me up and lowers me back down again, I duck my head underwater. I need to clear my head, not stare at the stranger. I came here to get way from a man. The last thing I need to do is get myself entangled with another one.

A dolphin nose pokes me in the back, but I resist. I deliberately turn away from the shore. I swim away from the dolphins, away from the man. Faster. And faster. I must get away. I swim until I'm out of breath. Tears fill my goggles, fogging my vision.

I may have thought I was healed, but I'm not. Part of me is still broken.

CHAPTER SIX

Luca

A few down days in this small seaside town helps me relax after weeks on tour performing nearly every night. Every morning, I run or walk several kilometers on San Francisco beach. The sea reminds me of Sorrento, Italy, the place where I grew up—a place I sometimes want to remember and sometimes wish I could forget. Creative thoughts flow to me whenever I'm in San Carlos. New lyrics flow into my mind the way waves roll over sand. I've noticed that my creativity stagnates after too many flights and time zone changes.

I lock my condo door and walk barefoot down to the beach. Small waves lap over the sand and barely a ripple disturbs the blue-green water. It's early morning—just past seven. The wind hasn't picked up yet, so the sea is still calm. I start to stroll along in the sand.

Next week, my band and I are doing the second leg of our *Estados Unidos* tour. The tour isn't sold out the way my tours in the UK and Mexico usually are. But I'm thrilled to be as popular as I am. Two of my recent albums went platinum in the UK, Mexico and Australia.

As a recording artist, romantic ballads and jazz fusion is my forte. I write lyrics and sing about love—being in love, losing love, finding love. Too bad my songs don't match my life. Twice, I thought I was in love. But each time I found out it was fame and money that attracted the women, not me. Whenever I sing songs of passion, of forever love, I see the face of the lover I haven't yet met, that I dream of one day meeting.

An American woman passing me on the beach greets me with a cheerful, "Good Morning." A black spaniel—free from a leash—bounds along beside her.

I breathe in a lungful of the salty air. During the week, the beach is largely deserted. Most people out on the beach now are out to walk early to beat the heat. It's usually only crowded on the weekends when American tourists and Mexican families from nearby cities come into town. Once I pass the rows of *condominios,* I continue walking along the undeveloped stretch of beach toward the El Soldado estuary.

The paparazzi haven't yet found me in San Carlos. When they do, I'll have to find a new place to decompress. They relentlessly pursue me whenever I'm on tour. They follow me to hotels, restaurants, and airports. Since I often sing about romantic love, reporters often ask if I believe that love can last forever. I answer, "*Sí*," even though all my life experience indicates otherwise. They ask if I wrote the lyrics for a girlfriend or someone I once loved. I say my songs aren't about anyone in my life now or anyone from my past. I tell them my songs of love have been composed for a dream girl I see in my mind. I believe she is out there somewhere. And I have every intention of finding her.

My mamá is the only real-life person that I sing about. I write songs to honor her and all she's done for our family. She knows the meaning of love. My mamá taught me that love isn't about getting what you need from someone else. It is about giving and being willing to make sacrifices for the sake of another. She brought my sister, two brothers, and me to Mexico City after my Italian-born father ran off with another woman. What was my mother to do? She was left alone with four children in a fancy house on the Tyrrhenian Sea with no means to support us. We were an ocean away from all her family. So, we left Italy and moved to Mexico.

Every night—until the night he disappeared—our father told us he loved us. My mother reserved those words for special moments. When she said, *I love you*, she meant it. My father's *Te amo*'s meant nothing. They were all lies. My mother never wasted time on empty words. She showed the depth of her feelings through what she did for us every day. She cooked our meals, helped us with our schoolwork, kept us clothed, and made sure all the bills were paid.

Meanwhile, my father was nowhere to be found. Once we arrived in Mexico City, we lived with my *Tía* Veronica until my mother found work as an office assistant. Then we moved into a cramped apartment, but we got by.

I step around a sharp shell on the beach. Three people are out in the sea kayaking. Another person glides across the water on a paddleboard. I'd try that, too, if I could swim. At least my sister, Chiara, got a chance to learn. And she's loved the water ever since.

My next *Estados Unidos* tour will be on the *Costa de California*. San Diego, Del Mar, Los Angeles, South Pasadena, and San Francisco. I just finished a tour here in my home country. It ended in *Cuidad de México*. My mamá now lives in a small town in the mountains called San Miguel de Allende. After so many years living in the chaos of the *Distrito Federal*, she wanted to be somewhere quiet. *Cuidad de México* is one of the largest cities in the world, hosting more than 20 million people. There are constant traffic jams, the air is polluted, and the streets are crowded and dirty. Large cities drain my vital energy. I felt exhausted after four days in the city. Breathing too much polluted air and hearing too many honking horns made me long to be back in this quiet seaside town again.

I turn toward the sea and spot another shape moving in the water. A dolphin perhaps? Then I realize, it's a person swimming toward the estuary, nearly at the speed that I'm walking. He's a really strong swimmer. Faster than my sister even. Maybe even an Olympian. Gliding through the water with a steady stroke and kick, seemingly unaffected by the rolling swells. Nearby, dolphins are arching out of the water and submerging. They appear to be headed directly toward the swimmer.

Does he know they're near? Is he afraid? I know I would be. They're so big. I stop walking and raise my binoculars to my eyes. I brought them for birdwatching in the estuary, but they should work well for dolphin-viewing, too.

I'm surprised to see it's a woman swimming out there. I know no man would wear that pink swim cap. She's surrounded by dolphins. Instead of the powerful freestyle she was swimming earlier, she's doing a slow breaststroke. She seems aware of the dolphins' presence and still appears to be relaxed. I see no signs of thrashing or panicky movement. A dolphin surfaces right beside her. I see two more dolphins not too far away. The woman lowers her head. She must be watching the dolphin underwater. Incredible.

The woman is fearless. It's almost like she knows these sea creatures. The dolphin beside her dives and soon is on the other side of her. She turns around to look at him and he dives again. He comes up behind her. Then he dives again and comes up so close, she could probably touch him—wait—I think she is touching him. I saw her reach for his back. She knows these dolphins. And these dolphins know her. How incredible it is to see someone so connected with these powerful, intelligent creatures.

Sudden longing tugs inside my chest. I've been drawn to the sea ever since I first laid eyes on this beach. I could be out in the sea, too, if only I knew how to swim. My childhood was full of worries once my father left. I was the oldest child. I went to school, worked part-time in the afternoon and evenings. I had no time for swimming lessons.

I imagine myself out there in the sea. I waded up to my chest yesterday and tried floating on my back. I enjoyed feeling my body rising and falling with the waves. But it would be so incredible to swim through the water like that mysterious woman out there. So effortlessly.

Como una criatura del mar (Like a creature from the sea).

The woman turns in my direction to look for one of the dolphins. And then follows it close to shore. I sense she sees me. Suddenly, I feel awkward. I've been observing her private moment. Basically, spying on her. I lower the binoculars and let them hang from my neck. She's swimming away from shore again. Almost like she wants to get away from me. I sense a hollow space inside of my gut that I didn't notice before. I wish she would have swum over to speak to me. Maybe she didn't because of my creepy behavior. I continue walking. But she stays in my thoughts. And then, the words to a song pop into my mind.

Every morning, I wake to a different place

Toronto, San Diego, Madrid, Rome

Another city, another concert, another place to sing and share my gift

It's who I am. I'm a performer. I sing songs of love. I sing songs of life

Sometimes I need to escape, to just get away

I return to this quiet seaside town in Mexico

My soul craves tranquility like the desert craves a drop of water

Here, I can remember who I am, I'm in a place where I can create

Chorus

Mysterious woman, she swims in the sea

So strong, so free.

Surrounded by dolphins

Surrounded by blue-green sea

She looks free.

The way I want to be.

I see her swimming in the Sea of Cortez, so fast and powerful

Like she belongs in the sea

Dolphins splash all around her

She moves, like flowing water, with them

In the sunlight she could be one of them

The dolphins must know her voice

A voice I'd like to know

I wish I could be out there in the sea, swimming free

Chorus

Mysterious woman, she swims in the sea

So strong, so free.

Surrounded by dolphins

Surrounded by blue-green sea

She looks free.

The way I want to be.

The lyrics play over and over in my mind. I hear the words in English, Italian, and Spanish. I perform in all three languages, depending on where I'm touring. I hum out the tune I heard in my mind as I composed the lyrics. I walk along considering the instrumentation. Acoustic guitar. Trombone. Saxophone. Drums. I've walked to the estuary and back, barely noticing my surroundings. But I still see the woman surrounded by dolphins in my mind's eye.

I look up, surprised to hear a splash. I was so lost in my thoughts I didn't notice the woman—no, not just any woman, it's her. The one I saw swimming with dolphins walks out of the water gracefully, revealing long tanned legs.

Her feet slide through the shallow waves without a hint of hesitation or difficulty with balance. She pulls off her goggles and swim cap and a torrent of wet dark hair tumbles over her defined, toned shoulders. Her eyes are large and dark and full of lively energy. She's wearing a pink and blue bikini. Every inch of her body is muscular and incredibly sexy. She swings her head suddenly in my direction, as if only now noticing me.

Oh, no, I'm staring. Again. At least this time it's not through my binoculars. What's wrong with me? I talk to women all the time. So why am I standing here like a frozen statue with my mouth hanging open? I need to say something before she runs away. "*Buenos días.*"

"*Buenos días.*" Her accent is distinctly American. Her broad smile and the happy lines at the corners of her big brown eyes show sheer joy. It radiates from her face.

I wonder if she is always this happy or if swimming in the sea with the dolphins brought that smile to her face. I change to English. "You're a very good swimmer."

She grins again and tucks a lock of hair behind one ear. "I've always loved to swim. But for many years I only got to swim in a pool. It's amazing being out in the sea."

"I'm sure it is. You're a very good swimmer." Already said that. I mentally kick myself. Let's try again. I clear my throat, feeling out of my element. I just repeated myself and I'm standing here looking like a prize nerd with binoculars around my neck. She swam away when she saw me earlier. I need to turn this conversation around so she doesn't walk away.

Que extraño (How strange). Usually, I'm trying to get away from women. They can be even worse than the paparazzi. They follow me into restaurants, into stores, laughing and giggling and handing me notes with their phone numbers on them.

One woman even followed me into a men's bathroom in a restaurant in Baltimore asking if I wanted to hook up. Now that's romantic. Sometimes I take someone to dinner and back to my place. But it never leads to anything meaningful. But no conversation I've ever had with any woman ever helped me prepare for this moment.

"Thanks. You should take a dip yourself—it's a perfect day for it." Her laugh is carefree. "I mean, after you put the binoculars away of course."

I lift the binoculars and let them fall back against my chest. "Yes, they would weigh me down a bit wouldn't they?" I pause. "But I don't swim." She's not asking me for anything. Not if she can go get her phone and take my photo or if I'd mind giving her an autograph. She doesn't strike me as the type to be obsessed with money or cars or expensive clothing. Maybe she's different? Someone I could enjoy going out with.

I've had enough of empty relationships where all the conversations leading up to the sex made me feel lonelier than ever. These women never asked about my childhood, or wanted to know about my mamá or my brothers and sister.

They asked how much money I make and if we could go for a ride in a limo. It's always fame and money women seem to be interested in, not me.

This sea swimmer seems different from any other women I've met. She's not only beautiful. She seems real. And being so near her sends bolts of desire through my body. Maybe that's why I can't say a single word that makes sense.

She tips her head and gives me a curious look. The long pause in our conversation has become awkward. I should say something. About the weather maybe. No, that's the kind of meaningless dialogue *no me gusta*. She saves me from having to speak. "Why don't you swim? You're uncomfortable in the water?"

"No, that's not it. I love the sea. I wade in to cool off. But I never learned how to swim." I'm appalled to hear the ring of sadness in my voice. I wanted a real conversation, which we're now having, but not for her to think I'm pathetic.

I pull my shoulders back, hoping a straight stance will make me look stronger and that it will boost my waning confidence. I already tower over this woman at six foot two. My shadow shades most of her body. My father and I have nothing in common in the way of values, but I can't change the physical resemblance. We both have a tall, muscular, Scandinavian-like body frame, probably since his great-grandparents were born in Norway.

She smiles and bites her thick lower lip in a way that's really cute. "I can tell you want to learn to swim. Why don't you take lessons?" Her gaze meets mine. She blinks once, then again. As if she's trying to decide whether she should say what she's thinking. Water drips from her long lashes. They make her eyes look so large and intelligent. "I guess I should introduce myself. I'm Jade." She extends a hand to shake, instead of coming closer for the customary Mexican kiss on the cheek.

I take her small hand in mine and shake it. Electricity races up my arm. My pulse hiccups. "I'm Luca. Nice to meet you." My gaze drifts from her face over the length of her body. Her body is strong and well-toned, but she has feminine curves in all the right places. Her breasts are large and round, her nipples teased to firm by the cool sea breeze. And she has the most amazing legs I've ever seen. Perfect muscle definition. Her thighs are beautifully shaped—her tan and the water droplets on them exaggerate each flexing muscle. And her calf muscles are incredible. Most women's calf muscles aren't even noticeable. But Jade's are curvy and perfectly shaped.

"I like that name, Luca," she says, slowly releasing my hand. "It's nice to meet you, too."

Now what do I say? I can't let this be it. I'm attracted to her and I want to know more about her. I could ask if she's staying at Bahía Delfin? But then she might think I'm only looking for a hookup. It would be nice to sit with her on the beach somewhere and talk. Swimming. I can ask her about swimming. "Do you swim every day, Jade?"

"Usually. Unless there's a storm and it's too rough. Then I have to settle for the pool."

"It sounds like you come to San Carlos a lot."

"I live here now. Moved down from the States a couple of months ago. How about you? Are you here on vacation?"

Her answer surprises me. Most Americans living in San Carlos are retired. Jade looks barely thirty. Maybe she got a work permit and started a business? Her comment opens up so many questions. I want to know how she ended up here. What she does for work. And if there's a boyfriend or husband in the picture. But I don't want to seem nosey. "Yes, I'm only here for four days. But I like San Carlos. I come here whenever I can."

I intentionally don't mention my career. She hasn't recognized me so far and I like being anonymous for a change. I've always wanted to have a normal conversation with a woman instead of having to answer the stream of usual questions. *What is it like to be a famous musician? You must love traveling all over the world. How much money do you make? Do you own a private jet?* I've had so many of these empty, shallow conversations without an ounce of real connection that I've lost count. When I'm on a date, I feel like I'm being interviewed for a feature article, "Pop Stars: They're Not Like You and Me."

"Too bad you can't stay longer." Jade looks out over the water, her eyes looking dreamy.

"You really like being out there, don't you?"

"I do. Swimming in the sea feels like a miracle every time."

"I wish I could swim." My shoulders and neck muscles stiffen. Why did I have to blurt that out? Again.

Her lively, intelligent eyes widen. They look huge surrounded by her long, wet lashes. "You could learn to swim while you're here."

"I've tried floating on my stomach and pulling with my arms, but I'm uncomfortable putting my head underwater and I can't do the breathing."

A broad smile brightens her face. "Maybe I can give you a lesson." Her voice rings with innocent excitement. She seems to have no idea what a challenge this might be.

"I don't know." She probably has a restaurant to run. Or a real estate office. Some workplace she needs to go. Her proposal is the perfect excuse for me to see her again, but I don't want to be a nuisance. And I would like to impress her, which I certainly won't do floundering around in the sea choking on water.

"How about tomorrow?" She glances at her watch. "Same time as now. You can meet me here at the beach. I'll teach you after my morning swim." She hands me her swim goggles. "I've got some extra pairs in my condo. Bring these along. Being able to see underwater might help you to relax."

I take the goggles from her hand, feeling another charge of energy when our fingers touch. "Thanks for letting me use these. And for offering to teach me." I pause. "Are you sure about this? I don't want to be any trouble."

She winds a long strand of wet hair around one finger and tips her head, studying me with her bright, dark eyes. The highlights in her wavy hair glisten in the sunlight. "It's no trouble at all,

Luca. I like to teach swimming. I wish that more people could experience what it's like to be out in the sea gliding over the waves."

"I should pay you," I blurt out.

Jade laughs. She touches me gently on the arm. "Don't be ridiculous. We're just having a bit of fun. I'm looking forward to it." She peeks at her watch again and a troubled look crosses her face. "I need to get back to my condo. I have a project due later that I need to get back to. I'll see you tomorrow."

"*Hasta mañana.*"

She takes a skipping step away, flings her wet hair over her shoulder and walks down the beach. I continue to watch her as she shrinks smaller and smaller in the distance. Jade may be a mile down the beach, but her footprints remain in the sand, a reminder that she's made a lasting impression on me.

CHAPTER SEVEN

Jade

My editing project is due in two hours. But my mind keeps drifting. I can't seem to keep it on task. My thoughts snap back to Luca. His blue eyes with a splash of green just like the Sea of Cortez. His thick, curly hair—tousled and messy. I kept wanting to brush a curl away from his eyes. The man has lips to die for. His mouth, surrounded by deep dimples, is so thick and sumptuous. I fantasize about kissing that sexy mouth of his, about touching those dimples, which deepen whenever he smiles. What's wrong with me? *No more men* is the game plan for my new life.

I swam away from Luca when I first saw him. Why didn't I just stay away? Complete insanity compelled me to swim back and talk to him. I've been just fine here on my own. Swimming, working, hanging out with my new friends, grocery shopping, and generally enjoying life without any romantic hassles to get in the way.

Why, oh, why did I have to get myself into this mess? I see one random, hot-looking guy on the beach and swim straight toward trouble.

Luca was dangerous enough from far away. He is large and powerful. Talk about ripped pecs. But up close, I sensed a vulnerability in him I didn't expect. And the chemistry between us is completely insane. Off the charts. His hot body and Spanish accent are hard enough to take.

Touching him pushed me over the edge. The instant we shook hands, a current of desire ripped through my veins.

I only talked to him for a few minutes, yet all these erotic thoughts about him keep racing through my brain. I imagine touching his face, kissing his distracting, swollen-looking lips. It's true, the man is damn distracting.

Any woman with a pulse would react to his looks. He could be a movie star or a cover model. Or an elite athlete with that powerful, muscular body. I'm sure he could be with any of the dozens of gorgeous young Mexican women on this beach. Instead, he was all alone—and seemed thrilled to talk with ordinary me.

I wipe Luca's exquisite face from my mind long enough to work through another ten pages of text. Then once again, my thoughts dance away from the screen. I offered to teach hot-looking Luca to swim. He'll be half naked. And wet. In waves that might knock him right into me. I'll never be able to focus. I can't focus now and he's not even near me.

I reprimand myself for my undisciplined thoughts. I need to finish this client's work. I'm a reliable and accurate professional who delivers her work on-time. Or at least I was. Now I'm a crazed woman with ADD. At least once I finish this project, I can do my morning swim. That's what I need now to clear my head.

I force my mind to stop going off on tangents and finish the last few pages of work. I compose an email, attach the document and click *send*.

Instead of the usual sigh of relief, I feel more anxious than ever. The project's done, but I still have the swimming lesson with Luca ahead of me. I can't wait to see him again. But I'm also stressed about it. Why couldn't I have chatted with him for a few minutes and then ended the conversation with "Have a nice day?" But no, I had to volunteer to give him a lesson after he told me his sad story about not knowing how to swim.

Damn it. I came here to avoid complications, not to walk right into another one. This day could have been like all the other days I've had so far here in San Carlos. Uncomplicated. Tension-free. But no, I had to make a mess of things.

I dash into the bathroom and slip into my swimsuit. I need this swim more than ever to rid my mind of all this turmoil. The male species has this amazing way of bringing turmoil into my life. Total chaos, actually.

I walk down to the beach, cap and goggles in hand. I gaze out at that blue-green water and hear the sound of waves rolling gently onto the shore. The sea calls to me. Every cell in my body craves immersion. I don't walk toward the sea, I run to it. My refuge. My safe place where I can escape all my worries.

The rush of water around me and the rhythm of my stroke will drown out what I'd rather forget. Brandon's rejection. The fear that I'm destined to be alone forever. The sea washes away those feelings of inadequacy. Nature doesn't criticize. Or judge. It accepts me as I am.

I wade deeper into the water. I can see the sandy bottom and a few dark strands of seaweed. I shuffle my feet through the sand in case there are stingrays, then start swimming once I hit hip-deep water.

I stroke over the swells until I'm about 30 feet from shore. Then I follow the contours of the coast, breathing every three strokes so I can see on both sides of me. The water on my face and head clears the haze in my brain and sharpens my thoughts to crystal clear.

Swimming feels like a miracle every time. The rays of golden sunlight penetrate the water's surface, illuminating tiny particles in the water. The sensation of the water flowing over my bare skin feels like a nurturing massage. Swimming in the sea is sensual, hypnotic. Already, this sea swim has smoothed away the rough edges of my emotions. They don't feel so overwhelming. The next stroke and the one after that are all that matter. I'm content now to be out here in the present moment, surrounded by this supportive, salty water.

My skin drinks in the sea's minerals and each time I turn my head, I breathe in the freshness of the salty, fresh sea air. The joy I feel swimming in the sea is hard to quantify. I want to shout out loud.

My swimming destination is the El Soldado Estuary. Whenever I breathe to the left, I see the terracotta structures of my condo complex along with an array of colorful tents, kayaks, and paddleboards on the beach. Whenever I breathe to the right, I see slices of volcanic landscape and a nearby island, but mostly open sea.

I transition from swimming freestyle to breaststroke. I look around for boats and other swimmers and to see if my dolphin friends are around. The place I live is called *Bahía Delfin* for good reason. Because this truly is dolphin bay.

Every day pods of dolphins gracefully glide along the shore, arcing out of the water for a breath and then descending again. Sometimes they're so far out, I see a flash of movement, blink and look again to see if I can distinguish a shape unique from the moving water. The endless sea teases my imagination, until every wave takes the shape of a dolphin or a sea lion. Freedom. That's what I experience in the water. I feel uninhibited, like the sea. And so alive.

Last night I dreamed that I stood by a glass window overlooking the sea. I saw a man swimming far from shore. Then I spotted a whale, but it wasn't the blue or gray I expected—the whale's skin was iridescent, like inside of an abalone shell. I wondered if the swimmer knew the whale was so close. He started swimming back toward shore. He stopped about twenty feet from shore, pivoted around and swam back out toward the open sea. But this time, he swam further and further from shore until I could no longer distinguish his shape from those of distant waves.

I wonder why I had that dream. Maybe because I, like that man, sometimes want to disappear in the sea forever. Or maybe I had that dream because the first time the dolphins dove underneath me, and I saw their enormous, powerful shapes underwater, my heart rate skyrocketed. I wasn't afraid, really. Mostly excited. But I wondered if I should have been scared. They're so much bigger and stronger than me. But I can't stay away from them. They're so fascinating. I love to be near the dolphins.

Scientists warn swimmers to be cautious around them. Dolphins are wild animals, they say. But people can be wild, too. Raping, killing, hating people for their religion or skin color. Dolphins must have different personalities just like people. How will I know if a dolphin is a nice guy or a fish with serious issues?

Below me, schools of silver sardines dart this way and that, confused by my presence. They should be more worried about the soaring pelicans. They glide so effortlessly on their lightweight wings. Their sharp eyes see movement and then they dive like a knife into the water, then surface, taking a sip of water to help wash down the fish. And then they swallow. That fish that was swimming one instant is in the bird's stomach the next.

A cloud of sand rises from the bottom. A startled stingray flaps rapidly away. The longer I swim, the more it feels effortless. My stroke flows with the rise and fall of the sea. My mind feels steady, content as I reach, pull and kick. The time has flown. It's five minutes until nine. I feel that familiar lurch of sadness. I experience it whenever it's time to leave the sea. There's work to get back to. Or shopping to do. And today, there's a man I barely know waiting for me.

Luca stands on the beach. I can't miss him—he stands out. He looks so strong and powerful, like a modern-day Hercules. The goggles I gave him are looped around one forearm and his muscular arms are crossed over his broad chest. He's only a distant silhouette from out here, but his posture looks rigid. Maybe he's anxious about the swim. Or maybe I make him nervous.

He certainly puts me on edge. I'm sure he'll look hotter than ever up close with his messy hair and Sea of Cortez eyes.

My heart beats faster. I hear the pound of my pulse underwater as I do a slow breaststroke toward shore. I can tell he hasn't shaved today. That shadow of stubble and his tangled hair—damn, why does Luca have to look so hot? My gaze traces over the slopes and angles of his face. He scrapes a finger across one dimpled cheek. Why is he so anxious? I'm no major distraction. My sister Kelsi would catch his attention for sure. Men always chase her. She's a bleached blonde, five foot nine, and rail thin like a runway model. She can get any man she wants, but never keeps them for long. She's no competition for me down here, but so many of these Mexican women on the beach are gorgeous. He can't possibly be interested in me.

Luca's a pleasant enough person. And he obviously wanted to learn to swim. It was completely adorable. How could I not to respond to that? But I need to wipe these silly notions from my brain about there being a spark between us. I'm not looking for a relationship anyway. I've already been there and done that. I definitely don't need to go there again. I came to San Carlos to start a new life, not to give another man an opportunity to rip my heart into pieces. I'll offer Luca a few stroke tips, wish him good luck, and then say *Adiós*. That makes sense.

What isn't logical is gawking up at him and conjuring vivid images of kissing and touching. But this view getting larger in front of me isn't helping support my stay-away-from-him case. My lust alarm bells ring louder and louder as I gaze at him through my goggles. My eyes are wide open and I'm trying not to blink because I don't want to miss a single second of this delicious view.

The morning sun shadows every bulge in his biceps, every smooth and perfect ridge on his chest and abdomen. I imagine skimming my fingertips over his chest, relishing every hard contour under my touch. My gaze wanders lower, to those happy trails of dark hair that follow the ridges along his lower abdomen until they disappear into the waistband of his form fitting surf shorts. I feel a spike of heat in my center and wonder what his weight would feel like moving over me. Oh, God, this is nuts.

Swimming lesson. You're going to give the guy a swimming lesson. I let a wave carry me into the shallows and then stand up. His tangled hair hasn't seen a brush today. He hasn't shaved. But Luca looks hot. So hot. I wish I could look that good with no effort. I feel self-conscious. I'm dripping wet and probably have seaweed in my hair. I hope to hell there's nothing gross hanging from my nose. I swipe at it quickly just in case. I just need to pull this off without sounding ridiculous. I want to sound smart and energetic and interesting. But right now, I feel panicky and inadequate.

"*Buenos días.*" I sound out of breath.

"*Buenos días*. I watched you swim for a while. You're an incredible swimmer." He flashes a heart-melting smile that deepens the sexy dimples around his lips and brings a twinkle to his blue-green eyes. It's like glittering sunlight on the sea. His hand darts out to steady me when a wave and an awkward hole in the sand cause me to stumble.

A shockwave of pleasure rolls through me. It's the second time he's touched me. I have no doubt I'll be flashing back to the nerve-igniting sensation of his touch all day. "Thanks."

His hand feels so strong and supportive. While I'm thinking how good his touch feels, his grip on my arm slackens. His hand drops back down to his side. I feel a jolt of withdrawal. His touch felt so good. I look at him for a moment, wondering if he felt anything too. If his skin reacted to the contact the way mine did. I can still feel lingering heat where his fingers gripped my arm.

He's focused on pulling the goggles over his eyes. Maybe he doesn't want me to read his thoughts. My gaze darts toward Luca's mouth. His dimples are deeper than ever, like he's clenching his jaw. He's anxious, that's for sure. If only I knew what about. I need to stop staring at his distracting lips and give some instructions. But I'm not sure I can even speak English let alone Spanish while he's just inches away.

His nearness has sparked a raging storm of heat in my body that is making my nipples tingle and giving me surges of hyperactive energy. I want to run, jump, turn a cartwheel. I clear my throat. "I'm looking forward to this. Teaching you to swim I mean." I shuffle nervously. "Why don't you start by showing me a few strokes of freestyle."

"You want me to put my face in the water?"

He told me yesterday he was uncomfortable putting his face in the water. I should have known better than to skip practicing that skill. "Yes. Why don't you try it standing first? Just duck under the water and blow air out through your mouth and nose so you don't swallow water. Then come up again."

"Okay, let me try." He takes a couple breaths first, puffing his cheeks out nervously before ducking underwater.

I see bubbles rise to the surface above his head. He comes up and pushes hair from his face. "That wasn't so bad."

"It was perfect. Now go down and blow your air out and come up and try to take a single breath before going down again. This will help get you ready for breathing with your stroke."

He nods. Takes a couple of breaths. Then he starts and takes five complete breaths before stopping. He breathes heavily after finishing. Obviously, he was anxious about it.

"That was perfect," I compliment him. "How did it feel?"

"Good. I thought putting my face in would be more difficult. But there's one problem." He wades into shallower water and pulls the goggles off of his head. His eyes are already ringed by suction marks. "Can you show me how to adjust these goggles? They're too tight. I tried to adjust them earlier, but I couldn't figure out how they work."

"Oh, yes, of course. I have a small head. And these are easy to adjust, but you have to know how to do it." These goggles—my favorite brand—have a release button to adjust tightness. No more pushing and pulling straps through awkward pieces of plastic.

My fingers brush against his as I take the goggles from his hand. The contact makes my breath catch in my throat. My will is strong. It's shouting loudly—stay away from men. But there seems to be no way to stop my body from reacting to his nearness. His touch—it's setting my skin on fire. "Just push this button," I say in a tremulous voice. "T-Then you can lengthen or shorten the strap. It's easy once you know how to do it." I demonstrate, showing Luca how to loosen and tighten the strap before handing the goggles back to him so he can adjust them until they feel just right.

Instead of adjusting the goggles, he just looks at me and smiles. I stare back for a moment and then snap my gaze away. I watch other people on the beach. Kids building sand castles. Toddlers throwing sand. Children and teens gliding on waves toward shore on boogie boards. I can't look at those blue-green eyes I could drown in. Why can't Luca put the damn goggles on already? Now I'm feeling bad for not meeting his gaze. I'm teaching him, not random kids on the beach. But the awkwardness makes me want to run away. I don't want to feel vulnerable like this.

Does he know how distracting he is to me? I'm standing here like a complete idiot dripping wet with a crimson face. Maybe he'll think my face is still flushed from my long swim. "Are you going to put on the goggles?"

He tugs on the strap and then tries on the goggles twice before he nods and says, "*Listo.*" Now that his eyes are covered, I find my gaze locking onto his lips.

Once again, I imagine what it would feel like to have those lips pressed against mine. A hot possession by that mouth would be incredible. If anyone had kissable lips, it's him.

Oh, God, what did I get myself into? Why couldn't this be just another normal day? By now I should be back in my condo showering, about to sit in front of the computer to start another writing project. I came to Mexico to start over. To keep it simple. To stay away from men. But that plan isn't working out well at all. I'm not only letting the enemy touch me, I'm letting him ignite my flesh and make my emotions go haywire.

My gaze wanders over the mounds of his chest and down the plains of his firm, hard abdomen, following the dark hair that leads my gaze toward his waistband and…oh, no, I'm not going there. Not going to imagine him naked. No way. If only my body would stop reacting to him like this. Every nerve ending in my body is vibrating with need. Swimming lesson. You're giving him a swimming lesson. I clear my throat and cross my hands over my chest. "Don't forget to shuffle your feet when you walk."

"Why? Are there stingrays?" His brows raise over his goggle-covered eyes.

"There aren't too many near shore when the water's warm. But it can't hurt to shuffle, just in case." I watch as he shuffles his feet into deeper water. I wonder if being out in this wild water will be scary for him at first. Many people are afraid of what's in the water. I've heard people scream if a fish brushes up against them. I better not tell him the fish around here like to nibble on toes.

Luca's expression looks more determined than anxious now, which is a good sign. As he wades out deeper, I wade along with him, wanting to be nearby in case he needs help. He's a guy after all. He's unlikely to admit he's in trouble. He's all rock-solid sinew and muscle. Even in this salty sea, he might sink straight to the bottom.

"Okay, now try a few strokes with your face in the water. But keep your feet down for now. Just lean over and practice. And remember to blow the air out through your nose and mouth." I demonstrate what he's supposed to do.

He leans closer to the water and practices a few strokes with his face in the water. Then without saying anything he plunges forward and tries to actually swim. He takes a few fast strokes, splashing water in every direction. He gasps and lifts his head straight up for a breath.

He's fighting the water instead of working with it. His arm strokes are much too fast. Like he's moving through air. He never gets a chance to even catch the thick sea water. He stands up suddenly, then sputters and coughs. "That didn't go so well. Maybe I should try again."

"It was a good start. A couple of changes will make it much easier."

He coughs again and gives me a one-sided smile. "I hope so because that was exhausting." He pauses, still breathing heavily. "I think I just swallowed the whole sea." He raises his goggles to his forehead and meets my gaze. His eyes, warm with laughter, flicker from blue to green and back again, the way the sea changes color with depth. His wet eyelashes cast shadows across the skin under his eyes.

Maybe when his thoughts and emotions shift, his eyes change color like that. Did he go from thinking about swimming to thinking about something else? Touching me, kissing me, sliding my swimsuit straps slowly from my shoulders... "Choking on water is never fun. I've done it enough myself. But a tweak to your stroke can keep that to a minimum."

"A tweak?" He laughs. His grin deepens the sexy dimples on either side of his mouth. He is so hot, sometimes I forget to breathe when I look at him.

"You won't inhale water if you slowly blow the air out through your mouth and nose whenever your face is underwater. Just inhale when you turn your head to breathe. Like this." I show him the head rotation. "When you lift your head to the front, rather than to the side, you're more likely to swallow water and your feet sink."

"There's too much to think about."

"Try humming whenever you exhale. It will keep a steady stream of air coming out through your nose and mouth."

I stand beside him. "Let me demonstrate again." I lean over the water, demonstrating the stroke with the head turn and breath. "And one more thing."

He laughs again and pushes some wet curls away from his face. "Only one?"

"You're being too hard on yourself. This next one is an easy fix."

"I like easy."

"Remember you're moving through water, not air. Try to slow down your stroke. That way it will feel easier and you will be working with the water, rather than fighting it."

"When you swim, it looks easy," Luca says.

"That's only because I've had years of practice. Now let's try it again. But just strokes, not with the breath to the side. Take a deep breath before you start swimming, keep your head down and take several slow, long strokes, exhaling air through your nose and mouth. Once you need to inhale, you can stand up."

He nods and repositions his goggles. Then he leans over and cups his hands bringing them near the water as he prepares to try again. I can't help noticing how good his torso looks wet, every contour exaggerated by the slick water sliding over it. His biceps flex and the broad muscles in his back contract as he prepares to swim. Then he launches himself off the bottom.

This time his strokes are slower, more precise. He's catching the water. He manages to take twelve long strokes before standing up. He obviously has good lung capacity.

He jumps up. Water drips from his thick dark hair, his chiseled face, over the taut mounds of his chest. His chest expands and contracts with each heavy breath.

"Is that better?" He looks at me for approval.

"Oh, yeah. Much better. You're a fast learner."

"And you are a good liar," he teases.

"No, I'm serious. Did it feel different when you slowed down your stroke?"

"It did, actually. It felt kind of good. Much more powerful."

"Excellent. Now we'll get to work on the breathing."

CHAPTER EIGHT

Luca

I've never felt so awkward in my life. *Lo que estaba pensando* (What was I thinking)? I meet this *mujer hermosa* who swims like a mermaid. And instead of asking her to dinner, I let her persuade me into taking a swimming lesson. That's a great way to impress a *señorita*. Letting her see up close what you're the worst at.

It's great that Jade doesn't recognize me and that she isn't giving me that star-struck look I'm used to seeing all the time. But this swimming scenario has swung things too much toward the opposite extreme. I'm splashing around and choking on water. *Sin control* (Out of control). She'll never want to go out with me now. I wish she could see me doing a weight workout or finishing an eight-mile run. That might impress her. I want to impress her more than anything right now.

Even wet, she looks *muy atractiva.* Once she finished her swim, she peeled off her cap and allowed her hair to fall free over her shoulders. Then she stuffed the cap and her goggles in the waterproof bag she wears around her waist.

My gaze keeps falling to her breasts. They're impossible not to notice. Her swim suit is stretched tightly over them, exaggerating their perfect shape. I keep imagining how their weight would feel in my hand, how their fullness would feel in my mouth.

I lick my lips, watching the cool breeze tighten her nipples. Damn. They're only inches away. But I can't think about nipples now. And how much I want to touch her skin. I need to listen to her analysis of my stroke and be able to apply it.

Basically, I need to blow up my swimming stroke and start over. Not that I'm surprised. Maybe this is hopeless. But my discouragement wanes when she offers a simple tip about slowing down my arm movements. That doesn't sound too hard. I might as well see how it works.

I try doing the slow strokes…and suddenly I'm actually moving. That turned out to be surprisingly easy. She tells me how great I'm doing. How did she do that? *Ayúdame tan rápido* (Help me so quickly). She managed to turn my discouragement into a triumph. Once I do the strokes to her satisfaction *tres veces,* she asks me to try the breathing.

"Try it first standing up," she suggests. She demonstrates again, what she showed me once earlier. Her lean arm muscles tighten as she pulls her hand through the seawater.

I stare at her in awe. She's incredible. She'd probably have endless endurance in…

"Remember three strokes and then breathe."

Her words snap me away from *mis pensamientos eróticos*. I try a few stroke cycles, leaning over the water.

Her hand grips my wrist, slowing down my movement. "Remember, slowly."

Searing heat rips through me. Every time she touches me, it's like lightning strikes that spot and then shoots like an electric current straight toward my groin. This chemistry between us is *muy intenso*.

The last thing I need is to finish this swimming lesson with an embarrassing *erección*. Jade seems so relaxed and in control. Maybe she's not feeling the same hot sensations. Meanwhile, I'm out of control. It would have been much easier to get to know her in a quiet restaurant over a glass of *vino tinto*. Maybe I'm swimming somewhat better than when I started, but compared to her, I'm *un desastre*. But I tell myself it really could be worse. She could be chasing me for my money and fame like all the other women I've known.

"Are you ready to put it together?" She issues a challenge.

I nod, feeling a surge of determination rise in my chest. "Ready." I take a deep breath and think about taking slow strokes before I start. I count in my head—*uno, dos, tres* as I swim along—and then I roll my head to the left and open my mouth to breathe.

But I forget to exhale underwater like she told me. So I have to exhale and inhale before I put my head back down again. I do a little dog paddle while I breathe and then try again. *Uno, dos, tres*—this time I blow out my air and I inhale like I'm supposed to. *Muy bueno.* I might as well keep going. I feel my body rising and falling over the gentle waves. The sea supports me even though I'm not kicking much. *Uno, dos, tres* —I turn my head, but a wave goes straight into my mouth. I tread water, choking.

Jade puts a hand on my arm. "Are you okay?"

Her touch makes me jump upright. I'm still out of breath and coughing. Some water has gone so far up my nose I can feel it in my forehead and ears. Talk about uncomfortable. This is the strangest workout I've ever done that's for sure. Physical discomfort blended with embarrassing awkwardness and a megadose of sexual attraction. I cough again and raise my hand and nod. "Y-yes. I'm fine."

The warm empathy in her large dark eyes makes my heart swell. She knows this is difficult for me. Her voice sounds soothing and compassionate. "Your swimming looked really good. Why don't you catch your breath for a few minutes and try again? If you feel a wave rolling toward you, try dipping the opposite shoulder a little. That way when you roll your head it will be higher above the wave and you can avoid swallowing water." She moves her arms and dips one shoulder and then the other to show me what she means. "I know it sounds hard, but it will come naturally with practice," she promises.

My gaze fastens on her lean muscled shoulders and upper arms. Her bright-colored swim suit exaggerates her tan. She's so strong and sturdy. I've never seen a woman with such toned muscles.

"Okay, let me try." I think about everything I need to do to get this right. Then I plunge in and start swimming. I drop my right shoulder down low when I breathe to the left. And it works. I take three more strokes and breathe again without choking on any water. That small feat feels like such an accomplishment. I keep swimming. I do two more breathing cycles before I'm too out of breath to continue. I stand up to see Jade's still right beside me waiting with a warm smile.

"That was fabulous. You really got it down."

"Thanks. It felt really good." I smile. Knowing that I've pleased her makes me feel that same swell of warmth in my chest that I experience when an audience gives me a standing ovation. Delivering a great performance matters to me because they're loyal fans. They've sacrificed time and money to see me. But this is different because I don't know my fans personally.

I don't know much about Jade either, except that every time she touches me, blazing heat surges through me. And so many things about her surprise me—*de la mejor manera* (in the best way). She's so natural and real. She could have emphasized everything I did wrong. Instead she's complimented and encouraged me until I was able to swim halfway decently, and I experienced a sense of accomplishment.

"Do you want me to do it again?" I say, even though I've had more than enough. The water feels like bathwater and the sun's beating down on my back. My muscles feel heavy and tired.

"No, I think that's enough for today. How about if we work on it some more tomorrow?"

"Sure. That would be great." I answer too quickly. I wonder if I sounded too desperate. There's something about Jade that just makes me want more. A lot more.

"Nine o'clock tomorrow then," she says.

"Jade, I really appreciate this. I didn't think I'd be able to do this. But you helped me to relax. And I actually enjoyed it." I reach into my swimsuit pocket for the money I sealed in a

Ziploc bag. "Please take this." I reach toward her hand.

She looks up at me. "Luca, really. I don't need you to pay me. I offered to help you because I wanted to."

"I know. But I want to. Since you spent so much time with me and I know you're busy."

She tips her head, looks at me for a moment and sighs. "Okay, I'll accept this on one condition."

"And what's that?"

"Tomorrow, I want you to come and let me teach you because..." She glances away for a moment and then meets my gaze. Flecks of gold appear in her large brown eyes. I see emotion in their depths. Deep emotion. That speaks so much louder than words. "Because I need a friend," she says softly.

For a moment, I forget to breathe. I keep thinking about the words she just said—and the significance of them. She wants to see me again. Does that mean she feels the same pulse-pounding sexual attraction I do when we touch?

CHAPTER NINE

Jade

My cell phone is ringing when I walk into my condo. The instant I answer, I wish I'd let it go to voice mail. It's my sister, Kelsi. I'm not in the mood to talk to her. I'm more in the mood to daydream—to flash back to what just happened out there with Luca. Or to take a shower and change. I'm still wearing a wet swimsuit. Goose pimples rise on my arms and I shiver, feeling chilled in the AC.

"I can't believe you're still down there," Kelsi says.

"Yep. I'm still here. How's Mia?" Mia's her four-year-old daughter. My sister's a single mom now. She and her husband split up two years ago.

"Okay, I guess. It sucks that you're not here to babysit on the weekends. I never get to go out anymore. But my sister has become anti-American. She'd rather be down there than with her own family."

"Kels—"

"Don't you ever get tired of being irresponsible?"

I roll my eyes and wrap my towel tighter around me. "I'm not irresponsible. I'm just happier living in this quiet place by the s—"

"Whatever. I thought maybe eventually you would listen to reason, but I guess that's not possible for you."

And she really wonders why I left? Our parents died in a plane crash when I was a freshman in college. Like Kelsi, they were critical and self-absorbed. They didn't approve of me choosing competitive swimming over playing a musical instrument. My dad went ballistic when he heard I planned to major in Creative Writing in college. There was no encouragement to go after my dreams. No recognition of all the awards I'd received throughout high school for my writing.

My father told me I'd be standing on a street corner asking for handouts once I graduated. He said he wouldn't pay for me to go to college unless I majored in engineering or business. I told him I didn't need his money, which wasn't true. I had applied for scholarships but hadn't been offered any.

My father was so angry with me. Once he vented and told me how rebellious and ridiculous I was being, he persuaded my mom to work on me. I eventually caved in and majored in structural engineering and managed to graduate magna cum laude even though nothing about the curriculum interested me.

Just last year, I put an end to the charade. I quit my job as an engineer, since for years I'd been publishing articles and books and taking online writing classes whenever there was time.

But I still found myself feeling like I had to explain myself to Kelsi and Brandon and too many of my friends.

Why I quit my job as an engineer. Why I thought writing was a worthwhile career. Why having a lot of money wasn't that important to me. I'd finish justifying myself—which I shouldn't even have had to do—and feel depressed and exhausted.

It was hard to have a decent self-image when people kept hammering away at me, saying that my gifts—swimming and writing—were completely worthless. Now I'm here in Mexico, trying to sew together pieces of me that have been ripped apart over and over again. I'll be damned if I'm going to let Kelsi destroy the mending I've done on myself so far.

"Living by the sea suits me. And I don't appreciate it when you talk to me like something's wrong with m—"

"Something is wrong with you, Jade. Can't you see? You live in a fucking dream world."

"I don't have to explain myself to you, Kelsi." But I start doing it anyway. "I have a place to live and enough money to pay the bills."

"You still write those books?"

I feel an uncomfortable pulse in my head. I wish like hell I'd never picked up the phone. "I'm not having this conversation."

"I know. You can't *deal* with it. And you'll blame me later if you get one of those migraines.

You'll tell everyone I 'stressed you out.'" I can practically see her hands making air quotes.

"Well, if there's no other reason you called other than to criticize me, I'm going to sign off now."

"Whatever. I wouldn't expect any different from you. You don't care about me or even about Mia."

"I asked about her right away when you called, but then you turned the conversation into a personal attack. I have to go now." Without waiting for her answer, I hit the *end call* icon on my phone and rest my head on the counter.

Why does Kelsi have to treat me like this? I left because I needed a change. I wanted to get far away from her and Brandon and be near the sea, which has always been my dream. Now I'm here in my new place and I'm happy. That's what I would want for anyone I cared about.

But not my sister. I'm sure if my parents were still living, they would have been livid, too. They never cared about what I wanted or what was best for me. I grew up loving to swim and write. They never watched me race—I always traveled to swim meets with my friends' families. And instead of congratulating me, they ripped me to shreds over the writing awards I won, saying I was wasting my time. Why is it that who I am is never enough for anyone?

I run back down to the beach as tears fill my eyes. I'm desperate to feel that sea all around me. To be in the only sanctuary I know on earth.

Ten minutes into my swim, I'm feeling better. Back in balance. The sea doesn't criticize. It accepts me as I am day to day. And it soothes away my suffering. I see the sleek flash of a dolphin's body in the distance. A few strokes later, I site in front of me just in time to see a line of fins just ahead. Then the group of dolphins dive underneath me.

Now dolphins are all around me, gliding by, releasing their loud, watery exhales through the blowholes on top of their heads before descending again. When two of them circle underneath me almost on their sides, I see their nearly white bellies underwater. I hear the force of air and water through their blow holes each time they ascend, their clicks and squeaks underwater.

Being near them makes me forget my suffering. I smile, I laugh. I feel joyful again. I don't know if they are happy and I'm responding to that or if it's something else.

Maybe it really is true that the sounds they make somehow balance human brain chemistry. Whatever it is, I want to sing and shout as happy emotions power through me. The shaky, upset me who hung up the phone 30 minutes ago has been transformed into a new me who doesn't give a damn what my sister or Brandon or my faux friends think. I'm the me I want to be right now, out here in this water with these awe-inspiring creatures, back to feeling light and free.

Two dolphins surface again. One has a large nick in its dorsal fin. The fin isn't quite vertical—it's slightly skewed to one side. Maybe something struck its fin from the side or it got caught on a fishing hook. The flaw doesn't detract from the beauty of the dolphin. I'm still drawn to him. Maybe battle scars don't mean a person or a dolphin is unlovable. They're what make him or her unique. "I'll call you, Nick," I say underwater. My voice sounds distorted. I wonder what the dolphins think of my underwater speech.

The response I get is a sound that resembles steady knocking on wood. I wonder what that means. Does he like his new name? But maybe this dolphin I've called he is actually a she. Nick could be Nic—short for Nicole—if the dolphin's a female. But everything I've read online indicates that male dolphins tend to fight. Maybe the fin got wounded in a skirmish and Nick is a boy dolphin after all.

Being near them makes me feel strangely calm. Watching them glide and jump and splash around brings a smile to my face every time. The dolphins are beautiful to watch. I've never touched any of them. Even though I've wanted to. But I worry if I did, they might perceive me as a threat. I wonder what a dolphin's skin feels like. Would it feel rubbery and slippery, like a swimming wetsuit? I hope one day I'll find out.

CHAPTER TEN

Luca

I wait for Jade to finish swimming. I'm going to ask her out. She wants me to—I'm almost sure. She got shy and nervous when she made that *friend* statement yesterday. She's attracted to me even though she doesn't know I'm famous and she saw me being the opposite of powerful and masculine—choking and gasping for air—while swimming yesterday. This says a lot about her. It proves she's drawn to more than just the image of me. She made me feel like it's okay to be imperfect. I don't have to perform any heroic feat to please her. I can just relax and be myself.

"Buenos días." She pulls her goggles from her head and skims off her cap in one smooth motion. Dragging her feet through the shallow water, she speaks in her familiar, jubilant voice. She's wearing a sunny smile and a pink and black competitive swimmer style bikini. Looking at her long lean wet body takes my breath away. Her swimsuit clings to her breasts and her flared hips, making me imagine peeling that wet suit off of her beautiful body.

"Buenos días. Como estás?"

"Excelente. The water's wonderful today. Are you ready to swim?"

"Por supuesto (Of course)." I pause for a moment. My gut clenches. I didn't think I'd be this nervous, but I want so badly for her to agree to see me later. I need to say this well, not jumble

my words all over the place. "But first, I want to ask you something." My voice sounds too serious. Like I'm about to ask for a quote on car insurance. I smile, hoping it will lighten the conversation. "I need to say this before I start choking and flailing around in the water."

"Okay." Keeping her wide eyes fastened on my face, she wrings out her wavy hair.

"Will you please have dinner with me tonight?"

She studies me for a moment, a doubtful frown shadowing her features. "Is this a sneaky way of trying to pay me for the swimming lesson?"

"No, not at all. Yesterday, you asked me not to pay for today's lesson—if I could just accept the lesson as your friend. And I said *yes*. Because I like being with you. I asked because I want to get to know you better. Oh, and to give you a chance to see me when I'm not at my worst."

Her lips perk up in a smile. Her cheeks redden. "You don't need to worry about that. You were fine. Most people don't have the guts to jump in and try something difficult. I like your persistence."

"*Gracias.*" The Spanish just slips out. I grind my teeth together. She hasn't said *Sí* yet. Is this a gentle way of letting me down? Asking again would be awkward. I decide to wait to see what she says.

She seems to sense my anxiety. She steps closer and places her hand on my shoulder. My skin burns with instant heat. My pulse starts to pound in my ears. "And as for your question… I'd love to have dinner with you tonight." Her hand slides down my arm to my hand. Her fingers interlace with mine. She smiles and tugs me closer to the sea. "But now it's time for you to swim."

More hot blood courses through my veins. Damn, the attraction between us is strong. No amount of coffee energizes me like this. Following her lead, I laugh and stumble in the shallow water. She laughs along with me. The playful nature of this interchange relaxes me. All the tension of waiting for an answer has melted away. She slowly releases my hand. She looks at me for a moment, blushing, then clears her throat. "Do you remember what we worked on yesterday?"

"Yes, of course." I position the goggles over my eyes and take a deep breath.

She asks me to show her some slow arm strokes first. Once I do that well, she has me add the breath to the side with the dip of the shoulder. When I put it all together, it feels surprisingly good. I watch the ripples on the sandy bottom moving below me as I propel myself through the water. I'm actually going somewhere. Before, it seemed like I struggled a lot while accomplishing *nada*.

"You're doing great, Luca. You amaze me."

"You're a great teacher, Jade. If you could teach me, you could probably teach anyone."

"You should give yourself more credit. You listen well and have been able to put all the pieces together. If you keep practicing, swimming will get easier and easier."

"I'll practice every day I'm here. I'll try to get to a pool when I'm traveling." We're standing in chest deep water beside each other. It feels strangely intimate to be alone with her in the water. Other couples are out in the water, kissing and holding each other. I wonder what it would be like to lift her up by the waist while the blue-green waves move around us, to taste the salt on her lovely lips.

"You should. It will help a lot."

I glimpse a dolphin fin out in the sea maybe 20 meters away. "Look, dolphins." I point in the direction where I saw the fin.

Jade shields her eyes from the sun and looks out over the water. "Oh, that's probably Nick and his pod. Do you want to get closer?"

My pulse beats faster at the thought of going out deeper. In the shallow water, I could stand up at any time. Near the dolphins, I'll be in water over my head and might feel helpless. "It's deep out there."

"Wait here. I'll get my buoy. You can clip it around your waist. If you get tired, you can just grab onto it and float." She dashes out of the water up to her beach tent and returns a minute later holding the bright orange buoy. "Are they still out there?"

"Yes, I just saw one jump."

"Great. Fasten this around your waist."

I take the buoy from her and clip it on. She explains that the buoy will trail behind me when I swim.

"Why don't you do three swim cycles of stroking and breathing out to deeper water and then we'll float there and wait for them. I'll swim right beside you."

"Sounds good."

I slowly propel myself through the water, the way Jade taught me and when I'm done with the three cycles, I don't feel as tired as I expected.

Jade pulls her goggles up onto her forehead and starts treading water, seemingly effortlessly. "How was that?"

I grab onto the buoy and float. "Fine. I wonder if they left. I don't see them anymore."

Jade claps her hands together and then says something out loud underwater.

"What did you say?"

"I said, 'Hey, Nick, it's Jade.' It might work. They know my voice. But they only come if they're in the mood to socialize. I don't know what they're up to right now. They might be feeding or playing games or mating."

"Can you tell what they're doing?"

"Sometimes. But I only saw fins—no tails or bodies—so I can't tell what they're up to at the moment."

Three fins emerge in front of us. I hear a loud, watery sound of the dolphins releasing air through their blowholes. Then they dive under again. They're coming right toward us. "*Dios mío.*"

"They breathe loudly, don't they?"

I put my head underwater in time to see enormous dark shapes pass underneath me. My blood pressure skyrockets. Fear constricts my chest. I never knew dolphins were so big. They must be three meters long. I paw at the water and gasp for air.

A steady strong hand grasps my upper arm. Jade's touch is both exciting and calming at that same time. She pushes the buoy that I'd released in my panic back toward me and I latch onto it.

"Relax. Just breathe, slowly. I know these dolphins. They won't hurt you."

I realize I've been hyperventilating. "Oh. It was a surprise. Seeing them." I take another breath. "They're really big."

The dolphins swim a circle around us, slowly, effortlessly gliding by.

"They're checking you out."

The water's so buoyant, all I have to do is slowly tread water to stay afloat. I put my eyes underwater to look again. They're swimming almost on their sides as if they want to get a better view of us. "I hope they approve. I'd hate to be smacked by one of those tails."

"That's how they stun fish to eat."

"That's comforting."

"It's all right, Luca. I promise. I'm here for you. Just relax and enjoy the moment."

She's right. I need to calm down. But this marine environment is her world. It's never been mine. To me this sea with its waves and currents and strange creatures is new. Although I find it exciting, I find it threatening, too, having these tank-sized animals so close. A fin surfaces right in front of me. Then it disappears. "Okay, where did you go?" I put my head underwater, but see nothing.

"He's trying to hide. Look behind you."

I turn around and the dolphin passes by me, just a few feet away. But it doesn't seem threatening. It's moving so slowly. Even though I've seen them swim very fast in the distance.

Jade's feminine voice tickles my ear, like the wind tickles my wet face. "They know we're fragile. That's why they move slowly when they're near us."

"I was just noticing that." I turn toward Jade.

She's smiling. Laugh lines surround her eyes. She's not the least bit nervous. Her dark eyes flash with joy, so alive and bright. They look at me with so much intensity that I feel heat rush through my veins. She seems so excited to be sharing this experience with me. I said I wanted to learn to swim. That I thought it would be *increíble* to be out in the sea with the dolphins. And she's given me both of these gifts—she's shared her world with me. "Oh, look! They're underneath us again."

I lower my head beneath the water to see enormous sleek bodies, drifting along beneath us. They have long noses and broad flat tails. And they're making sounds. Very strange sounds. I could touch them if I wanted to. But I don't want to. Not today.

"Trust me," Jade whispers.

She knows I'm nervous. And she's trying so hard to make me feel comfortable. I allow myself to enjoy this experience that I longed for since I first saw her out in the water. Out here, floating on these blue-green waves, smelling the salt air and feeling the sea breeze on my neck and shoulders, I'm closer than I have ever been to any sea creature.

The dolphins could just swim away, but they've chosen to spend time with us. I haven't felt this alive in so long. Being out here with Jade is like a dream. I love looking at her gold-flecked eyes, at the water glistening on her cheeks and her curvy, kissable pink lips. She's kind. She's compassionate. She sets my skin on fire. She even seems in-tune to my emotions. And this *bonita señorita* said *Sí* to seeing me tonight. This is the closest thing to romantic love that I've ever experienced.

CHAPTER ELEVEN

Jade

He'll pick me up at seven. My stomach is jumpy and I'm so nervous. So far, Luca's only seen me as a wet mess. Tonight's my chance to show him I can look good. I started getting ready more than an hour ago. I figured that would be plenty of time. But I keep wanting to do one more thing. I've changed dresses three times. Then I added more gel to get my hair to behave. Now I'm outlining my lips and about to roll on lipstick. I look at my reflection in the mirror when I finish and smile. My lips feel strange with lipstick. Lately, I haven't worn much in the way of makeup. I make a conscious effort to relax my lips and look natural.

Why am I so worked up about this date? I shouldn't even have said *yes* to it in the first place. I was doing so well—staying away from men. Then Luca showed up and now he's all I can think about. The man's constantly on my mind.

The knock on my door makes me jump even though I expected it. I release a loud exhalation. He's really here. My heart beats faster and my skin starts to tingle. I rush to the door and open it.

My eyes widen when I see how hot Luca looks. The scent of his aftershave hits me hard. Heat spikes through my body. "Wow. I mean hi," I blurt out. A warm smile spreads over his face, deepening his dimples. Two days of sun have darkened his skin. His wavy hair is tamed slightly with gel, which makes it look still wet. Super sexy. He's dressed neatly in khakis and an off-white dress shirt, unbuttoned enough to show off a swath of tanned chest and a sprinkling of dark hair. I feel stupid at first for gushing over him, but realize from his expression, he seems as pleased with what he sees as I am. I see a flicker in his eyes, like the diamond flash of sunlight on the sea.

"Hola. You look beautiful, Jade." He says it all in Spanish. His accent and his deep voice makes every word sound like a caress.

My heart skips around inside my chest. The look of appreciation he's giving me makes the time I spent getting ready worth it. "Thank you."

"You ready to go?"

"Oh, yes, of course."

As I walk beside Luca to his car, he tells me about the seaside restaurant where he'll take me. It's on the other side of town. Past the Bahia, next to Algodones Beach. He's renting a Volvo SUV. It's really comfortable, with leather seats. During the drive, he asks me more about my writing work. I tell him about the romance novel I plan to publish later in the month. The two articles I have due next week. And the intermittent editing products I take on.

I ask him about his career. He's quiet for a moment. He presses his lips together and his jaw muscles tighten. He looks strangely sad. I wonder why. I consider asking but decide that might be too intrusive. He glances toward me and tells me he travels often for work. He helps with stage setup for plays and concerts, he says.

"That sounds like fun. Do you enjoy it?"

"I do. I've met a lot of interesting people and have traveled all over the world."

"That sounds wonderful. I've always wanted to travel, to see more places." Too bad Brandon never wanted to go to Costa Rica or Greece or Bhutan. But Brandon's history. I have a new life now. I can do whatever I want and go wherever I want to go.

Luca turns off the main road and drives down a dirt road that leads to the sea. He parks the car.

Before I have a chance to open my door, he's there opening it and reaching for my arm. With his gentle support, I step down onto the ground. His touch leaves me feeling giddy and lightheaded. I push the SUV door shut. His hand skims down my arm to my hand. Our fingers interlace so naturally. We walk, still holding hands, through the sand into the outdoor restaurant. I can't help smiling. A happy tingle electrifies the skin on my face, spreading from my cheeks to my ears.

We walk past the bar and into the main restaurant area, which is all open toward the sea and topped with a thatched roof. A waiter in jeans and a T-shirt with the restaurant logo greets us in Spanish. Luca answers and the man leads us to a table.

The waiter pulls my chair back. I sit down and let him help me scoot in closer to the table. I lean back in my chair and admire the view. We have a great view of the sea, the curving coastline and two nearby islands. "What a perfect spot."

"I'm glad you like it." Luca sits beside me, rather than across from me, so we're both able to enjoy the sea view. We angle our chairs in toward each other so we can look at each other when we're talking.

The waiter returns to take our drink orders and returns moments later with the margaritas we ordered, chips and salsa, and menus. There's a pause in conversation while we decide what to order.

"Where do you live when you're not visiting San Carlos?"

"Nowhere, really. I travel so much for work, I just rent a place wherever I go unless I'm staying with family."

"I guess that makes sense with your schedule being so crazy and all. Where are you from?"

"I was born in Italy."

"Italy? You're far away from home."

Luca presses his lips together and shakes his head. "No, Mexico is very much my home now. We moved to Mexico City when I was still a boy. After my father abandoned us." He drops his gaze. I can tell it's a painful memory for him.

"Abandoned you. Oh, Luca, that's terrible. I'm so sorry."

He meets my gaze. I see a flash of determination and defiance in his eyes. He's a strong man, accustomed to dealing with adversity. That became crystal clear when I saw how he handled the swimming lessons. "You don't need to be. It was a long time ago. The five of us managed just fine on our own. My mom always put our family first. She did everything to take care of me and my sister and brothers. She's always been there."

"It sounds like your mom's an amazing person. Does she still live in Mexico?"

"Yes. She lives in San Miguel de Allende now—a quiet town up in the mountains. It's not too far from Mexico City."

"How about the rest of your family?"

"My brother, Lorenzo, works with me. My youngest brother, Nicolo, and my sister, Chiara, still live in Mexico City."

"That's great that you work with your brother."

"Yes, the two of us have always been close. But I can't for the life of me get him to come to San Carlos. He's got this thing for Vegas. He's usually there anytime we get a break." Luca shakes his head and laughs ruefully. "But that's not my scene at all."

"It's not mine, either. I find the place depressing." Naturally, Brandon loved it. He enjoyed the gambling, the glittering lights. He didn't seem to notice what I saw—people who clearly struggled with money frittering away their life savings, as they played the slot machines robotically. I felt sorry for them. "Do you get to see the rest of your family often? It must be hard to with your busy travel schedule."

"Family has always been a priority. I visit my mom every month. A lot of the time, Nicolo and Chiara meet me there. I also get together with them whenever work takes me to Mexico City. How about you? Where did you live before you moved down here, and where is your family?"

I pause to drink more of my margarita, hoping the tequila will give me the courage I need to tackle this more-than-a-little awkward question. Many Mexican families come to the beach on weekends to hang out. Grandparents, moms and dads, aunts and uncles all gather together. Some of the adults sit on the sidelines, talking to each other or drinking beer while others are in the sea swimming or splashing around with their children or helping them build sandcastles.

Many of the moms even wade into the sea in street clothes—jeans or flowing dresses or shorts. The wet clothes stick to their skin and look uncomfortable, but the women don't seem to care. They're still laughing and talking and enjoying everyone's company.

Watching how happy they seem together jerks at my heart strings and makes me realize what I've missed out on. All my grandparents passed away when I was in elementary school.

My parents have been dead for more than ten years now. My dad was adopted, and my mom's sister died of a drug overdose before I was born. All that's left is my sister, my niece, and me. And I have nothing in common with Kelsi. The sound of her voice is almost enough to make me break out in hives. Luca will think I'm pathetic. Disinterested in family. Not the kind of woman he wants at all.

"Is something wrong?" Luca's voice sounds gentle and soothing, and the look in his eyes says he's genuinely worried.

"It's hard for me to talk about it, that's all."

He reaches for my hand and gives it a squeeze. "Don't worry. We don't have to talk about that now if you don't want to."

"It's okay. I'm ready to tell you." I take a deep breath and resume talking. "I lived in Tucson, Arizona before I moved here. But I didn't leave much behind. My parents were killed in an airplane crash when I was a freshman in college. And my older sister and I—we're not close." I don't mention my niece. She's four years old and a really cute kid. But because of the strained relationship I have with my sister, I rarely see her. That bothers me. It bothers me a lot. But I don't know how to fix it. Being around my sister—talking to her even—is toxic. And I just can't put myself through that right now.

"I'm sorry." He releases my hand and is quiet for a moment.

I hold my breath, wondering what he's thinking. Probably how to let me down easily after what he's heard.

A Mexican-Italian man like Luca would want to be with a family-oriented woman. Not some loner with no one who came to Mexico basically because she had no life where she came from. "It's okay," I say, breaking the silence. "I've learned to become independent. I get by fine on my own."

As I say it, I realize it's true. Sort of. I am independent. I'm adventurous. A good problem solver. And I like to have quiet time by myself. But even now that I know how wrong Brandon was for me, sometimes I'm still lonely. When I first got here, I always went to restaurants alone. Restaurant hosts would ask if I was waiting for someone. I usually had to explain more than once—no, it's only me. Because everyone here has dozens of family members they can spend time with, they probably found it difficult to understand how anyone could have no one to eat with.

Ten days after I arrived here, I met a lovely Mexican couple—Gabriela and Martin—that I often join for long beach walks. Sometimes they even invite me to their home for dinner. They refer to me as their *hermana* or sister, which means a lot to me.

But Gabriela has four sisters and a brother living in San Carlos and Guaymas and she and Martin are so busy with family—and I'm kind of the odd one out, not being married. I tell them not to worry if they don't have time to get together. They always brush off my insecure comments and say they enjoy my company. We do always have fun together. They're such kind people, I hope they don't only hang around me because they feel sorry for me. If only I could let go of these fears.

"You look so sad, Jade. Please, tell me what you're thinking." Luca's voice is so gentle. He covers my hand that's resting in my lap.

"It's just..." I don't know how to answer without sounding foolish. And the last thing I want to feel is vulnerable so soon after what happened with Brandon. "My answer just feels so inadequate. And it makes me feel bad. I know how important family is to most people in Mexico. And I can tell how important family is to you. I'm an American with no one. I'm not the kind of person you should be interested in."

He takes hold of my hand and draws it to his chest. "That's not true. You are good, Jade. I can see that. It is not your fault that you are alone. I'm sure the longer you are in Mexico the more friends you will make. They will make you feel like part of their families. And you won't be alone anymore. You will be with people who value who you are."

My heart swells with emotion hearing his words. How did he do that? Make me feel so much better. His kind words have washed away some of my insecurities. "I hope that's possible."

"It is, you will see. No one is lonely for long in Mexico. People here take care of each other."

"Thank you, Luca for being so understanding. That was hard to talk about."

"You can talk to me about anything, Jade. I'm here for you."

I fight back tears, but this time they're happy tears. I've never been around anyone more thoughtful than Luca before. He just…he really gets it. "Thank you, Luca."

The waiter approaches to take our order. He speaks to Luca in Spanish.

Luca turns toward me. "Have you decided what you want?"

"I was looking at the shrimp dishes. But I'm not sure which one to get."

"If you like coconut, the coconut shrimp here is really delicious. That's what I'm ordering."

"I'll try it, then."

Luca orders for both of us in Spanish and then gazes out over the water, his face pensive. "Beautiful evening."

The sun slowly descends toward the horizon, illuminating the bay and painting the shore a brilliant reddish-orange. "It's lovely, Luca. Thank you so much for bringing me here. This is such a treat."

"The pleasure is all mine. I feel very fortunate to have met the most beautiful woman in all of San Carlos."

Cozy warmth burrows deep inside of me. He says such heart-melting things. Any woman would react to his words, especially when they're said in that delicious Latino accent. How do I know if this is part of his regular seduction routine or whether he means what he's saying? "You're just being nice."

"No, Jade, that's how I see you." He gazes at me without blinking, and golden fire flickers in his eyes.

Heat rushes to my face and I glance away. I see the lust and maybe even longing burning in his eyes. I don't know what it means. Or even if it's real. All I know is that I want more of it. I want more of him.

CHAPTER TWELVE

Luca

Color floods her tanned cheeks. My compliment made Jade feel awkward I can tell. Which is surprising. She's *muy bonita.* Surely, other men have told her that. She seemed so casual and in control on the beach. Tonight, I'm sensing a vulnerability in her I never expected. It's sad that her parents are gone and that her sister doesn't understand her. It hurts to hear that she feels so alone. I feel compelled to protect her, but she seems so anxious and I'm not sure how to get her to relax. I'll ask her more about her swimming—something I know she loves. "When did you learn to swim?" I'm gratified to see her eyes brighten and her lips turn up in a smile.

"I started lessons when I was five. Then I joined swim team when I was nine."

"You raced?"

There's a gleam of confidence in her dark eyes. "Yep. I was pretty good, too."

"That doesn't surprise me in the least. What events did you swim?"

"The 500- and 1650-yard freestyle and the 400 Individual Medley. The medley is the race that includes all four strokes."

"I knew that, actually. My sister, Chiara, is also a swimmer."

Jade's voice pitches upward with excitement. "Really?"

"Yes. After we moved to Mexico City, she kept talking about her one friend, Marisol, who swam on a team. She was only ten at the time. I was fifteen and had a part-time job. I persuaded my mom to let me use some of my money to pay for her to take swimming lessons. Eventually, Chiara swam well enough to join the team with Marisol. She really enjoyed it. She was great at the butterfly and breaststroke events."

"How wonderful, Luca. It's great that you helped her get started. Does Chiara still swim?"

"Now she swims for fitness. And she's the head swimming coach at the Pan American University in Mexico City."

"How awesome. You must be very proud of her."

"I am very proud of her. She found this sport she loves so much and made it into a fulfilling career. And she loves the water. In some ways she reminds me of you."

Jade tips her head slightly and bites her lower lip. "What do you mean?"

"I can see how much you love the water. I saw a similar flicker of delight in my sister's eyes every time she talked about swimming or an upcoming race. In so many ways, swimming changed her."

"What do you mean?"

"Chiara was moody and withdrawn after our father left and wasn't doing well in school. That all changed once she started swimming."

Jade nods. "I'm glad swimming helped your sister get through all that." Her eyes well up with tears. "I know I couldn't have made it through so many things that have happened without the comfort of the water."

I lean in closer to her until our shoulders touch. I want to hold her, but it seems too soon. "I understand, Jade. I know what swimming means to Chiara and what it means to you."

"I know you do." Her large dark eyes look at me so wide with appreciation. "I like that you get why swimming matters to me. That you don't think it's silly."

"Why would I? Your love for the water is one of many things that makes you unique and special."

The sea breeze blows a lock of her curly hair into her eyes. My fingers itch to reach out and brush it away. Before I get the chance to touch its luxurious softness, she pushes the hair aside, revealing the smile it had hidden. "You see things so differently, Luca. My sister thinks I'm a complete nut. I get so tired of having to explain myself all the time. That's one of many reasons I came down here."

How could anyone not like her? I barely know her, but already I can't get enough of her company. "You ran away from people who didn't understand you?"

"Basically." She pauses for a moment, as if deciding whether to say more. "But it's a bit more complicated than that." She looks up at me with those big brown eyes like she'd hiding a guilty secret. "I was in a relationship with someone for eight years. Then he dumped me. In my favorite restaurant in front of a bunch of people. It was the worst."

I clench my fists, feel a wrench of anger rise in my chest. How could any man treat her like that? I place my hand on her bare shoulder, savoring how smooth and soft her skin feels. "Oh, no, Jade, that's terrible. I can't believe that."

"I was devastated. I felt stuck in a rut and wasn't sure how to get out of it. One night on Facebook, I found these expatriate groups. People who had moved to other countries posted and commented about their experiences. The idea of going someplace new thrilled me. I thought, why not? I knew I didn't want to run into Brandon at the grocery store. And my new career as a writer meant I could work anywhere with a steady internet connection."

"You say you could have gone anywhere. Why did you choose Mexico?"

"For a lot of reasons. I wanted to live by the ocean and I wanted to live someplace where life was more relaxed. And Mexico was close. I figured I could bail if it didn't work out."

"I can tell living by the sea suits you. How do you like the lifestyle?"

She sips her margarita and licks a grain of salt from her lips. "I love it, actually. The pace is slower. It's easier to make friends here. I don't feel like I have to prove anything to anyone anymore. I got so tired of having to explain myself."

I know she has more to say so I wait for her to continue.

"Last year, I resigned from my job as a structural engineer to start writing full time. Even when I was just writing at night and on weekends, I made a decent amount of money writing books and doing freelance writing and editing. I saw no need to continue work I didn't enjoy. Everyone told me I was crazy. Brandon—my ex—and my sister were the worst. How could I give up a real job? A steady job with benefits? Oh, and my 'status?'" She rolls her eyes as she makes a quotation mark gesture when she says the word *status*. Lines of distress crease her forehead.

No wonder she wanted to come here. If these people really cared about her, they would want her to do what made her truly happy. Thanks to their harsh words, she's obviously really hard on herself.

"This career change was what you wanted, wasn't it?"

"Yes. I'd had enough of working nights and weekends every time a deadline loomed. I wanted my life back. The company owned my life more than I did."

"I can understand why you made that choice."

"I wish my boyfriend and my sister had been so sympathetic. They pestered me to death about it. And then..."

Her eyes well up with tears. She hurriedly wipes them away.

I ache to pull her into my arms, but the timing isn't right. It's obvious she's been bruised and battered, and I don't want to scare her. Maybe she's still getting over the breakup with her boyfriend. Not that she should think of him for a minute longer.

The guy is obviously an insensitive jerk. I need to be a good listener right now. Give her the time and space to learn to trust again. I hope I can win her trust, but it might take some time.

"That's terrible that the people closest to you were so critical. It took a lot of strength to stand up for yourself and to make the choice that worked best for you. I want you to know—you never have to explain yourself to me."

A long sigh escapes Jade's lips. "Thank you, Luca. I appreciate that. I wish I could let all that crap from my past go. But it's hard sometimes."

"I understand. I got into quite a bit of trouble when I was a boy. I was a real practical joker. Especially in lower secondary school. The administrators didn't find the firecrackers I threw under their door amusing. That stunt landed me a two-week suspension. And there were other incidents. I've often thought if I hadn't been such an unruly kid, maybe my father never would have left."

Jade's eyes widen in surprise and she reaches for me and touches my shoulder. Her fingertips brush down my arm, leaving a smoldering trail of heat behind. "Oh, no, Luca. You must know now that's not true. Nothing could make a parent who truly loves his child walk away. You were just a mischievous boy."

I want more than ever to pull her into my arms—to express how much it means to me that she not only listens, but she also understands. And she's been so misunderstood herself, which amazes me. She's so compassionate and kind—I would think everyone she meets would like her right away. She's living in my country now and I want more than anything to make it be a safe place for her, a place she can truly call home.

CHAPTER THIRTEEN

Jade

Luca rakes a hand through his thick hair and gazes at me. His eyes are more blue than green now. I wonder what he's thinking. Too Much Information, probably.

It was bad enough I had to tell him about my pathetic family life, but then I had to blurt out what happened with Brandon. No guy wants to hear about a girl's ex. But I couldn't stop myself. I said it without thinking, which isn't like me. I tend to keep my emotions to myself. There's just something about Luca. He makes it feel safe to let it all out and I really needed to talk about it. At least our conversation wasn't one-sided. He opened up to me, too. We both suffered when we were kids. And that makes me feel closer to him. He understands the pain of rejection.

Luca's skin is tinted orange by the setting sun. His eyelashes are tipped in gold. But he doesn't try to shade his eyes from the sun. He continues to study my face. Time seems to stand still as we look at each other. His stare heats my skin. The physical and mental connection between us seems to make the air crackle.

The crash of the waves on the sand and the music with the loud backbeat suddenly fade away. All I see is Luca. All I hear is the sound of my own breath. My heart beat intensifies. I know what the flash of warm light in his eyes means. He wants to get to know me in a more intimate way.

I keep thinking about what I want—and what I don't want. I want to be near him. He says nice things, but I don't know for sure they're really true. He's always traveling. What if he meets someone else in New York, London, or Rome. No. This won't last. I'll just get hurt again. There's no way I'm going to sleep with him tonight. Even though every nerve ending in my body is screaming for me to give in, to allow myself this indulgence.

Our gazes break apart when the waiter brings our plates to the table. The shrimp is cooked just right. I savor a bite, chewing slowly. "Great suggestion. This is delicious."

"I knew you would like it."

We exchange small talk over the food and how nice it is outside. There's only a hint of yellow-orange in the western sky now and stars are popping out in the midnight blue sky. If ever there were a romantic evening, this is it. I never expected to enjoy it so much. I keep thinking about what might happen after we leave. Will he try to kiss me? How will his lips feel on mine? What will it feel like to be embraced by those strong arms of his, to be compressed against his rock-hard chest? I shouldn't be fantasizing about kissing him, imagining him teasing one of the straps of my dress off one shoulder and touching my breast.

Getting close is dangerous. There are so many reasons I shouldn't give in, but neither my mind nor body can resist him. My mind wants him because he's so kind and thoughtful. My body wants him because every inch of his muscular body is gorgeously sculpted masculine sinew. I don't have to give in to these impulses, but damn, I want to. Every time we touch, that undercurrent of sexual awareness pulses through me.

I love how different Luca is from the other men I've gone out with. He hasn't bragged about his high IQ or how much money he makes or how much weight he can bench press. Some of the stories men have told me make me laugh. They want me to believe they'll be the next Bill Gates. Somehow, they never seemed to realize that money and status don't impress me. All I want is a connection. Luca has focused his attention on getting to know me instead of wasting time telling unbelievable stories and trying to show off.

When dinner is over, Luca drives me back to my condo. He holds my hand as he walks me to my door. Each step feels heavier than the next. This night was so wonderful, and I won't see him for a while. He's going back to work tomorrow.

He turns to face me when we reach the door. Every perfect angle and feature of his face is illuminated by my porch light.

I imagine reaching out and stroking his cheek. "I had a really good time."

"It was lovely spending the evening with you, Jade. I hope we can see each other again when I come back."

"I would like that very much."

"Do you have your cell phone?"

"Yes, it's in my purse." I unzip it and sift through all the junk until I locate it. He gives me his number and asks me to text him mine. Once that's complete, he flashes a heart-melting smile. My pulse beats faster. He wants to kiss me. Oh, please, yes.

He leans in toward me. "You look so lovely. I've wanted to kiss you all evening," he says softly. "Is that okay?"

"Yes," I say in a whisper. My belly quivers as I wait in anticipation for his mouth to descend. His lips brush against mine, like a feather at first. Shivers cascade all the way down to my toes.

Then I feel the full shape of his mouth against mine. The warm wet meeting of our mouths sets my whole body on fire.

His hands skim around my back as he pulls me closer. I melt into the magnetic pull of his body. He deepens the kiss and a groan of pleasure escapes my lips. The press of his hard, powerful body excites me. A bolt of desire moves through my body. Then, when I start to sense the swell of his arousal pressing against my thighs, he releases me. Slowly. Gently. He gazes at me and says softly, "I will see you soon, Jade."

"See you soon," I say to him as he disappears in the darkness. I stand there for a moment wondering what happened. And wishing more than anything he was still there.

CHAPTER FOURTEEN

Jade

The sea flows over my skin and I swim along the shoreline, urging my mind to relax, but it refuses to listen. I keep thinking about Luca. It's been a week since he left. I gave him my number, but he still hasn't called. Every time my cell phone rings, I check the caller ID to see if its Luca. Instead, it's the office calling to let me know they need to turn the water off for two hours. Or Gabriela asking me to dinner. Each time I hear the phone and see that it isn't him, despair washes over me. I miss him so badly.

I know I shouldn't put my life on hold waiting for him to call. He told me he traveled a lot almost right after we met. I knew it would be like this. I don't know why I expected it to be different.

He'll always be busy working, and I don't want to be sitting around waiting for a call that will never come. This isn't what I need now. I'm not secure enough not to be imagining the worst.

One minute I'm thinking he hasn't called because of my miserable family situation. The next I'm wondering if he's talking to a gorgeous woman, resting his hand on her arm, gazing at her intently with those blue-green eyes like she's the only one that matters—the same way he looked at me.

It's too awful to think about. Too shattering. I want to be the only woman he looks at. But how could I be? I'm so ordinary. Oh, God. All I wanted was to be able to live with myself, not to go back to picking myself to pieces all over again.

When I near my end of the beach I swim toward the shore and shuffle my feet through the shallow water. As I step out of the sea, I strip off my cap and goggles.

My ears are filled with water, but I hear a man's voice like I'm hearing it through a tunnel. I turn toward the source of the sound. If only it were Luca. But it isn't. The man standing near me on the shore has pale skin and a lanky frame. He's got a military-style crew cut and is wearing a polo shirt and khaki shorts.

"Hi, there." His voice sounds whiny. Annoying. His lips are twisted into a disturbing smirk.

I instinctively don't like this guy or the way he's staring at my body. There's something about him that rubs me the wrong way. And I'm in no mood for chit chat. "Hello."

"Hi, I'm Justin. I can see you like to swim."

Great. That certainly sounded stalker-ish. "I do, actually." I don't bother to tell him my name.

"I don't know why you swim near those dolphins. They can be mean. How much do you weigh?"

"What?" Is this guy for real?

"They must be at least ten times your size. You'll end up getting hurt." His condescending tone instantly grates on my nerves. Why the hell are people always telling me what to do? Do I have a sign pasted on my forehead saying, *I'm dying to hear your unsolicited advice*?

I try to walk around the man, but he steps in front of me. I look up at him and give him my best hostile stare. "Thanks for the advice. I'll bear that in mind."

"You think you're tough. But those animals are big. They could hurt you or even kill you."

"But they wouldn't. I know them. They're my friends."

A smirk curls up one side of his lips. "They're wild animals. You're so naïve. I read online that male dolphins sometimes try to rape female swimmers."

I put my hands on my hips. He wants to argue? Fine, let's do it. "Really? So your point is that some dolphins are aggressive and mean. So are humans. A lot of them can be much more dangerous than any dolphin I've met out in the sea. And some of them are just annoying." I fall short of saying, *Take you for example*. "Now if you'll excuse me, I've got work to do."

"What kind of work do you do? Someone mentioned you stay here all year. There's no money to be made down here."

So he's been gossiping about me with other people. Nice. God, this guy grates on my nerves. I try again to step around him, but he grabs my arm as I pass. "How about dinner tonight?"

When hell freezes over. "No, thanks. I'm busy."

His laugh sounds sardonic. And cruel. "Busy. In this place? You're joking. I've been here for two days because a coworker said she loved this place and already I'm bored senseless. I can't wait to get back to my orthodontics practice. It's very successful. I'm so busy I'm not even taking new patients."

Like I care. Why won't this creeper leave me alone? Isn't it obvious I don't want to talk to him? "Let me spell it out to you, then. I'm seeing someone else." I twist free from him and storm up the beach.

"You're making a mistake," he calls after me.

"Yeah, right," I mutter under my breath, fuming. I walk up the beach. Instead of feeling relief at escaping the creep, I feel a heavy sadness settle in my chest. What if the orthodontist's right? What if the dolphins I hang out with aren't the nice creatures I imagined them to be. Maybe once they get to know me, they won't be so gentle anymore. Maybe they'll play rough with me or try to sexually assault me. I tell myself it's not possible. They wouldn't do that to me. Not my dolphins.

I wish Luca were here. He'd understand my fears and be willing to listen. He'd help me get some insight into the situation. But he'll be gone for two weeks. I wonder why he wouldn't share more about his work with me? Maybe I'm being naïve about him too. I don't really know him any better than I know the dolphins. I never even asked Luca his last name.

CHAPTER FIFTEEN

Luca

I'm in the limo with the guys. We're on our way to Observatory North Park in San Diego, the site of tonight's concert. Whenever I'm on stage, I think of Jade. She's been on my mind ever since that night we had dinner together. I can't stop thinking about that kiss we shared afterward. And how soft her skin is. But it wasn't just the attraction flaring between us that's been on my mind. She really listened to me. I see her smile and her heart-shaped face, framed in shimmering waves of chestnut hair, each night before I fall asleep. Every time I see her in my mind's eye, a thrill of energy races through me.

"Is there anyone there?" My brother Lorenzo says in Spanish as he snaps his fingers in front of my face. He plays the saxophone in our band.

"Thinking about that girl again?"

"What made you think that?"

"Because you have that sappy look on your face. Did you think I wouldn't notice?" He fidgets with his cross pendant and shakes his head.

I've always been honest with Lorenzo, but I wish he wouldn't tease me so much sometimes. *"I miss her."*

"Have you called her yet?"

"No. Our schedule's been crazy. There never seems to be a good time." The real reason I haven't called Jade is I don't know what to say. If she asks me about work, I might say too much. I

really need to explain all this in person when we're together.

"That's not it." Lorenzo scratches his beard and gives me a penetrating look. *"Oh, I get it. She doesn't know, does she. Who you are, I mean."*

I had to know he'd read it right on my face. *"No, not yet. She was talking to me like a normal person. That never happens with women."*

"What did you tell her?"

When I explain that I told her I'm a tech guy for concerts, he frowns and shakes his head. *"You have to tell her."*

"I know. And I will. But it has to happen when we're together."

"I understand. Maybe you could call when you know she won't be there and just leave a message."

Of course. I could call Jade sometime while she's out swimming. *"Good idea. I don't know why I didn't think of that."*

"Probably because you're too busy thinking about her naked," Lorenzo smirks.

"Stop it."

"I can tell by that dazed look on your face that it's true."

"I've been thinking about the new song we're performing tonight. Jade's Song."

"The audience will love it. You really outdid yourself with this one, brother. I can tell this woman has sparked something in you."

"She has." Will this song about my beautiful mermaid swimming with dolphins have relevance to people listening in our audience? I want them to experience the gamut of emotions that Jade makes me feel. To grasp the profound effect she's had on me.

She's ignited my creativity and made me feel that it isn't impossible for a woman to genuinely take interest in me. I know our relationship is new, and that maybe I'm getting my hopes up for no reason. But Lorenzo's right. I have to tell her who I am. Soon. I almost told her before I left her at her door. But our kiss was like nothing I've ever experienced before. I didn't want to ruin the moment.

Lorenzo grabs his cell phone from his pocket. *"I need to return a call."*

All the guys seem to be absorbed in texting and surfing the internet on their devices. I wonder if I could Facetime her real quick. To let her know she's on my mind.

I recall how patient she was with me during the swimming lessons. I almost said *no* to her offer of a second lesson. I felt guilty taking so much of her time, especially when she said she wouldn't take any money. She had work to do. But I could tell she wanted to see me again, and that the attraction between us was mutual. That sizzling heat burned hotter and hotter the more we were together.

Her stroke suggestions made me see that even a small change would fix everything. The strange thing about her tips—they did make a night and day difference. Because she believed I could do it, it seemed possible.

I pull my phone from my pocket. Try to call Jade's number on Facetime. I'll tell her we're on our way to an event, that I only have a minute. I bite my lip, anxiously waiting for her to answer, hoping she'll be happy to hear from me and that she won't ask too many questions.

I can't lie to Jade. She deserves to hear the truth from me when I'm there with her, not when I'm hundreds of miles away. When I get back to San Carlos, I'll walk down to the beach and find her after her swim. And then we'll talk. The line continues to ring, but there's no answer. Feeling defeated, I disconnect and drop the cell phone back in my pocket.

My trombone player, Raphael slaps me on the shoulder. "We're there. It's almost showtime."

I jump up from my seat. "Ready."

Raphael laughs, his white teeth barely visible below his thick moustache. "It didn't look like it for a minute there. You looked like you were in a distant galaxy."

"Just running through the words to the new song, that's all."

The driver opens the door for us. Security at the venue keeps the fans from approaching the vehicle. Once we're outside, we stride toward the back door that leads to the stage.

"And the girl the song is about, I'm sure," teases Raphael.

"Jade, the dolphin woman," Steve, my drummer, chimes in.

Obviously, they can't resist ribbing me since they've never seen me this interested in any girl before. "You'll never know."

"Lorenzo already told us all about her."

"Brother, I'm going to have to hurt you," I say, punching him affectionately on the shoulder. Tonight's the night I'll be sharing Jade's song with the world. She told me Mexico is the right place for her to be now. If only I can convince her that I'm the right man for her. Maybe she thought so that night we had dinner and shared that passionate kiss. But will she still feel that way when she finds out who I really am?

CHAPTER SIXTEEN

Jade

I leave my condo, geared up and ready to swim. There's a plain envelope on my doormat. I frown. I wonder what it is. I pick it up and rip it open. How strange. Inside is a clipping from a newspaper. It's a computer printout of an article from the *San Diego Union-Tribune*. Why would someone drop this by? I wonder who delivered it. My mouth falls open in shock when I study the photo accompanying the article. "No way," I say out loud. Because I'm looking at a picture of Luca.

He's holding onto a microphone, up on a stage illuminated by bright lights. Behind him are four band members. I read a few lines of text—about all the performances he's given, the multiple Grammy awards he's won—and then I have to lean on the door for support. This is the stage set up he's been doing in California?

He never said a word about being a musician. Why didn't he tell me he was a pop star? This is crazy. He tried to call me on Facetime last night, but I was at Gabriele and Martin's house then and missed his call. I was ecstatic beyond belief to know he'd tried to reach me. I managed to connect with him later. He looked adorable on the video. And as always, he said heart-melting things. He said it would only be four days until he got back. That he couldn't wait to see me. And I've been dying to see him, too. Until this. This is what I came to escape—the disconnect, the lies. It upset me when I didn't hear from him for so long. Somehow, I forgot the sleepless nights the instant I found out he'd tried to reach me. But he intentionally lied to me. It's just not right. Why didn't he want me to know the truth about his career?

Last night when I asked him what venue he was preparing for, he said he was setting up the stage for a Justin Timberlake concert. Why couldn't he have told me the truth? How hard would it have been to say he was a musician? That he was the one performing.

I know he's not the type of guy inclined to brag. He didn't have to tell me he had record-setting crowds attend his performances. Or to tell me he's one of the wealthiest men in Mexico, which he is, apparently, according to the article. But to leave me completely clueless? That's just wrong. I don't know Luca. I don't know him at all.

I toss the printout onto the kitchen table and leave the condo. I stomp through the sand toward the sea, yank on my swim cap, and pull on my goggles with a frustrated huff. This is all my fault. I shouldn't have let my emotions run away with me. Vulnerability is weakness, one I can't afford to indulge in.

Right now, I need the sea. My only sanctuary. Only the blue-green Sea of Cortez water can smooth away these miserable feelings, the anger and betrayal that threaten to cripple me. I rush into the water, desperate to escape. My normal protocol of shuffling my feet is forgotten. I cry out when a sharp barb of a stingray strikes my foot.

CHAPTER SEVENTEEN

Luca

I'm back in San Carlos three days before Jade's expecting me. I want to surprise her. I could tell by our Facetime conversation that she missed me. I can't wait to see her. I keep imagining her bright smile, her golden-brown eyes lighting up with excitement when she sees me. I can't wait to show her how I've progressed with my swimming. Pools were everywhere in California, so I was able to spend time practicing my stroke every day in addition to maintaining my regular running and weight lifting routines.

I've worked up to swimming twenty lengths of a hotel pool without stopping. Okay, maybe that's not great, but it's a big improvement over wearing myself out in only ten strokes.

I walk down to the beach at the time I usually see Jade swimming. I spot her immediately, out in the water, but I don't see the dolphins. There's something different about her stroke. She always looks strong and powerful when she swims. But now she's swimming so fast. Like she's racing or being chased by a shark. Maybe she's training for a race? Her stroke looks almost angry. Could she be upset about something?

A man strolls toward me on the beach. His arms swing wide of his torso, the way a man with bulky biceps would walk. But this guy looks like his upper body never lifted any serious weight—he's skinny and pale and his chest is slightly sunken in. His twisted grin irritates me. I nod and say, "Good morning" anyway to be polite. He doesn't answer.

As he walks past, he turns toward me. Instead of offering a friendly greeting, he says, "You're not going to try to swim with those crazy dolphins, are you?"

I resent the nosey question. "I'm thinking about it."

"Don't you have anything better to do?"

I like how people engage in casual conversation in this small town, but this guy is trying to bait me. I grit my teeth and try to be polite. "Not really. I'm on vacation. I'm here to enjoy the beach."

"Must be a letdown after being on tour."

I let out a nervous laugh. *Que terrible*. I was hoping I wouldn't be recognized so soon in this one place I've found to relax. "I need a break just like anyone else."

"I know—you're here to see the girl? Too bad she found out who you are. She was so upset she went in to swim yesterday without shuffling her feet and got stung by a stingray."

Jade hurt? My muscles constrict in anxiety. I turn toward the water, wishing she was here on the beach instead of way out there. I want to hold her, talk to her, make sure that her wound is okay and no longer hurting her. "Oh, no, that's terrible. Was it bad?"

The man raises his chin in an arrogant way and nods. "I was on the beach when it happened. I rushed over right away to help her." He emphasizes the word, *I*, in a way that makes me want to punch him.

He was here when she was injured instead of me. Jealousy pierces me sharply in the chest. I don't want to think about this mean-spirited man touching her foot or any other part of her body. But she was in pain and needed someone. Y *yo no estaba ahi* (And I wasn't there). Even worse, I was the cause of her distress. If she hadn't been overwrought, she would have shuffled her feet like she always does and wouldn't have been hurt.

"Women don't like to be lied to. I thought she deserved to know the truth."

I clench my fists and grind my teeth together. "You told her. Why? I was going to tell her. I just needed some time."

"I bet you did." He smirks and walks past me.

My chest feels tight—I'm so frustrated. I never meant to deceive her. I just wanted a chance to get to know her without my fame getting in the way, a chance to tell her when I felt like the time was right.

What I wanted was unrealistic. I rolled the dice and took a risk by trying to hide my life from her. I knew the odds were stacked against me. And I lost. Now she probably won't ever speak to me again. I put on my goggles and wade out in the water. Maybe I can find calm in the water like Jade. All I want right now is to clear my head, to get some perspective on the situation.

Should I keep my distance? Or try to talk to her? If only she could understand what was behind my silence. I needed to know if it was me she was attracted to—or just the image of me.

And now I know. She agreed to a date, not knowing I was a celebrity. There must have been something about the real me that caught her attention. That still amazes me. Every other woman I've been involved with lately has been obsessed with my celebrity status. It's such a turnoff. I could tell Jade genuinely liked me.

I swim parallel to the shore, toward the estuary in the direction I saw her swimming. She's out of sight now. She swims so fast, I'll never catch her. But I might see her when she's on her way back. My stroke feels relatively relaxed compared to a week ago. The changes she made to my stroke helped and the practice has paid off. The water is salty and buoyant, it's no effort at all to stay on top of the water. It feels easy compared to the pool swims.

I keep swimming parallel to the shore, hoping I'll see her. Maybe she'll be so impressed that I'm out here practicing, she'll forget her anger and give me another chance. Noticing that my arms feel heavy and fatigued, I roll over on my back and take a few breaths, looking up at the clear blue sky. And then I keep swimming.

But I never see her. I don't see the dolphins either. I roll over on my back again to rest. I glance at my watch. I've been in the water for almost 30 minutes, much longer than I've ever swum before. On the way back, my limbs start to feel heavy. I can barely raise my arms out of the water to take a stroke. I shouldn't have swum this far. It's really hot today. The water feels like warm soup and I didn't drink enough water for this long of a swim. I'm dehydrated and fatigued.

I can make it, I tell myself. Just a little further. I start angling toward shore. That's when I see Jade on the beach. Talking to that *imbécil* who approached me earlier. She's waving her arms in the air. She swipes at her eyes with one hand. She's crying. Upset. Because of me. He leans in toward her. Places a hand on her arm. The hand drifts down to rub her back.

No. She can't be involved with him. He's not right for her at all. She needs a strong man. That guy's nothing but a ten-pound weakling. Even worse, he's vindictive and rude. He's not the kind of guy she should be hanging around. I tread water and watch them.

A wave splashes into my face and fills my mouth. I cough and choke. The adrenaline of watching him touch her distracted me. Now my body screams that its completely spent. I cough again. Another wave splashes me in the face, and this time goes up my nose. What am I going to do? I'm still at least twenty meters from shore. I frantically stroke my way through the water to make it to the beach. My view underwater starts to tip and sway. It's just the waves, I tell myself until I realize I no longer have the strength to lift my head out of the water.

My body slowly descends toward the sandy bottom. No, I say through the water. I see a trail of bubbles and hear the sound of my distress. And then as my brain grasps that I'm not going to make it out of this alive, I wish somehow Jade could end up with a good man. Someone who really cared about her. Someone who could protect her. I feel something rubbery moving underneath me. And then I see only darkness.

CHAPTER EIGHTEEN

Jade

Justin's hand touches my back. I flinch at his touch. I don't want his hands on me. The guy creeps me out. But I'm overwrought. I'm riding a rollercoaster of emotions. I should tell that I just want to be left alone.

"It's better that you know. That's why I g—"

His whiny voice breaks into my thoughts. It annoys the hell out of me. I take a step back, my hands on my hips. "Wait, you put that article outside my door?"

One of his pale brows lifts. "What if I did?"

Sudden anger heats my face and I lean in toward him, willing myself not to punch him. There's nothing I hate more than people meddling in my life. "You're crazy. I don't even know you and now you think you can run my life? You say I shouldn't swim with dolphins and drop off a newspaper article about my boyfriend to try to mess up our relationship."

"Oh, he's your boyfriend now, is he? He's definitely not a very good swimmer." Justin cranes his neck toward the sea.

"What do you mean?" I turn around to see what he's looking at. There's a man struggling in the water. Oh, no. It's Luca. I could identify his stroke anywhere. His left arm always comes straight up out of the water on the recovery. But he's not supposed to be here. Not for three more days.

I shield my eyes with one hand to block out the sun. I watch him pause to tread water. But his movements look frantic. His chin is barely above water. He's paddling fast with his hands and splashing water everywhere. He's exhibiting all the signs of being a drowning swimmer. His head sinks lower and disappears under the water.

I drop my cap on the sand and sprint into the water, shoving on my goggles. I dive in and swim toward him. I'm almost there when I see my dolphin friends. Two of them are trying to nudge Luca toward the beach. Nick is underneath him, preventing him from sinking to the bottom. I swim toward them, but I don't try to take over. They move much more quickly than I could.

In less than a minute, Luca's in waist deep water. I step in and the dolphins glide away once I scoop Luca into my arms. "Thank you, Nick. And all of you."

I drag Luca from the water and stretch him out on the sand a few feet away from the gentle surf. Tears fill my eyes and pain twists in the pit of my stomach. Will I be able to save him? I pull the goggles off of his head and turn my ear to listen to his chest to check for breathing.

He starts to cough up seawater. Then his eyes fly open. They look more gorgeous than ever. Blue with a hint of green and rimmed with big lashes that are wet with sea water. I forget that I was mad at him for not telling me he was a famous singer. He's alive and that's all I care about right now.

I fling my arms around him and kiss him on the lips. "Oh, thank God. you're okay. When I saw you out there, I…" His lips feel so cold. I kiss them again, trying to bring warmth into his body. "Why? Why did you swim alone like that?"

A faint smile raises the corners of his beautiful mouth. "I wanted to surprise you."

CHAPTER NINETEEN

Luca

Jade kisses me again. Water from her wet hair drips onto my face. Her dark eyes are full of tears. She cares. She didn't kiss me because I'm famous. She kissed me because she was scared she would lose me. She's not crying because if I'd drowned, she'd never have a chance to ride in a limo. She's crying because she's thrilled I'm still alive.

I ache to touch her, to pull her in close and crush my lips to hers. But I'm so weak from my struggle in the sea that my muscles refuse to move. They feel heavy and leaden. All I can do is lay in the sand and admire her beauty. I look up in awe at her wide-open eyes framed with wet lashes, her wet hair that is glued to her face and her slick wet shoulders.

I try again to raise my arm, but I can't. I sigh with frustration, then I allow my muscles to relax and sink into the sand. I almost drowned. Of course, I can't do much at the moment. I need to rest. At least it's not over. I didn't die. And she appears to have forgiven me. There should be many days in our future when I can kiss her and hold her. "I'm sorry I didn't tell you." I hear my voice inside my head. One of my ears is still clogged with water.

"We'll talk about it later," she says. "Let me see if I can find someone to help me get you to your condo. What unit are you staying in this time?"

She speaks again before I have a chance to respond.

"Oh, wait, you better come back to my place so I can make sure you're okay."

"Please, just let me rest here for a minute." I turn my head and notice the beach is mostly deserted. No one seems to have witnessed my near drowning. There was that irritating man I saw talking to her, touching her. I wonder where he went.

She glances around. "I thought maybe Justin could help me carry you. He was here a minute ago, but I think he left."

Hearing the mean man's name on her lips boiled his blood. "He's not a good person. When I came down here to swim, he rubbed it in my face that he'd told you about my career."

Her brows draw together. "I know. He was a jerk to do that. But I'm still upset that you lied."

"Jade, I'm sorry." If only I could touch her. But my muscles are still too weak. "I know it was wrong. But it's complicated. I really enjoyed that night we went out and those days at the beach. No woman ever has shown any interest in me without knowing I was famous. I wanted a chance to just be a…a person." All the talking leaves me out of breath. The inside of my mouth feels like its lined with sandpaper.

Her lips open wide and a surprised "Oh," escapes her lips.

I remain silent and watch her. I can see by the slight inward tilt of her brows and the emotion in the depths of her dark eyes that she gets it.

My head feels like it's tumbling backward. My view of Jade's face blurs and then starts to sway. I feel dizzy, overheated, and desperate for a drink of water. I see more shapes moving around me. And then I hear a man's voice. "Do you need help?"

"He almost drowned," says Jade. "And I think he's dehydrated. Could you help me move him to my condo?"

"Maybe we should call Rescate." The man pulls a cell phone out of his pocket. "They can send an ambulance."

"No," I say in a weak voice. "I don't need an ambulance."

"They're a volunteer medical group. It wouldn't hurt to let them look at you."

"No, please, I just need some water and to get out of the sun." Struggling, but finally able to move, I push myself up and rest back on my hands. My view of the sea sways. A wave of nausea sweeps over me. I don't think I can make it to my feet.

"We'll help get him inside then. I'm Thad. And this is my wife Amanda." Jade quickly introduces herself and tells them my name. I feel supportive hands on my arms and shoulders, raising me from the sand. The bald-headed man studies me curiously.

"Hey wait. I thought you looked familiar. I've seen your videos on YouTube. You're Luca Espinoza, aren't you?"

I give Thad a weak nod, leaning heavily on him and Jade as I stumble my way through the sand toward the condominium complex. Moving brings some strength back to my muscles. I work harder to support more of my weight. By the time we get up the stairs into the grass, walking doesn't feel so bad.

Still holding my arm with a tight grip, Jade turns toward me with a worried frown on her face. "You shouldn't be exerting yourself."

"I can move better now. *Está bien.*"

Thad supports me again as we walk up the stairs. His grip on my arm tightens. "I've got him. You go ahead and open the door."

Jade unlocks the door and pulls it open. "Come on in. Let's get him onto the couch."

My body is still covered with sand. Worried I'll make a mess of her tidy condo, I lean over and attempt to brush it off.

"Don't worry about it," says Jade. "I'll just brush enough sand off so you won't be uncomfortable." While the couple supports me, she skims her hand over my back and shoulders. The jolts of sensation her touch incites is a pleasant reminder that I'm alive.

The three of them walk me over toward the couch. I collapse gratefully onto the leather cushions. Jade raises my head to place a pillow under it.

"Thank you so much for your help." I raise my head and then let it drop again. The long walk has drained all my strength.

"It was no problem," Thad says, adjusting his wire-rimmed glasses, which are slightly askew after the difficult trip up from the beach. "Maybe we can get a photo with you later?"

"I can do better than that. How would you like tickets to one of my concerts? I'll be performing in Hermosillo in October."

Thad looks at Amanda with surprised eyes. "Really? That would be wonderful. We're in condo 262."

"I'll print out some for you and drop them by later."

"Don't worry about that now. Just rest." The two of them stand beside the couch, watching me curiously.

Jade comes closer and leans over me. She's wearing her swimsuit and has a floral sarong knotted around her waist. She's carrying a tall glass of water. I take it from her hand and drink it all down in a few gulps.

"Would you like more?"

"*Sí, por favor*. It tastes really refreshing."

"I put a dash of coconut water in it. For some electrolytes."

"*Buena idea.* I'm sorry I keep speaking in Spanish. I'm still disoriented."

"Don't worry, Luca. It's okay. Hang on—I'll be right back." She takes my empty glass and heads back into the kitchen, returning seconds later with more water.

"Well, we better be going," says Thad. "Please let us know if you need anything."

"I sure will. Thank you again," says Jade. "It was nice to meet you."

I thank the couple for their help and then allow my head to collapse back on the pillow once they've left. I should get up and go back to my condo. I don't want to be a burden to Jade. But I'm so comfortable. My back slowly sinks deeper into the leather cushions, my eyelids drift closed. It's a comfort to know Jade is nearby to check on me.

She smooths her hand over my forehead. "Why don't you rest for a while."

"I don't want to cause you any trouble."

"It's no trouble at all. I wasn't planning on going anywhere anyway. I'll be at my computer, working on a project. I'll be close by if you need anything." She has that look in her eyes, like she doesn't want to step away.

"I'll never lie to you again, I promise."

"Hearing Thad ask for a photo after you nearly drowned made me understand why you didn't reveal who you are. It must get old to be recognized everywhere you go."

"It is. But the loneliness—that's the worst. I get along great with my brother and the other guys in our band. But dating has been a nightmare. I've always wanted to have dinner with a woman who actually likes me."

Her eyes widen with compassion. "You have obviously been asking out the wrong women."

My insides melt in response to her gentle tone of voice. "Obviously. Until I met you."

A blush creeps up her neck and reddens her cheeks. "That's nice of you to say. I do like you, Luca. Very much." She leans in closer. Her face, her lips are just inches away. Her skin smells of salt and coconut sunscreen.

My lips tingle in anticipation of the kiss. I reach for her face and stroke her soft cheek with my fingertips. "Thank you, Jade. For saving me. And for understanding."

"You're welcome." She hovers over me for an instant and then shifts away. "I have work I need to do. But I'll be right in the next room if you need me." She pats me on the shoulder and steps away.

I do need her. More than she knows. But the kiss that never happened tells me she's still afraid. That she's still afraid I will hurt her.

CHAPTER TWENTY

Jade

The sun slowly descends toward the western mountains near the jagged volcanic peak of Tetakawi. I shield my eyes from the glare, which is heating up my living room more than I'd like. The sun disappears, leaving behind its signature on the horizon—setting every feathery cloud on fire in brilliant hues of orange, pink, and red.

Luca is still sound asleep on my couch, snoring softly. I walk over to him and study his face. My fingers drift toward him, but I resist the temptation to stroke his face. His thick brows and dark curls and even the dark shadow of his day-old beard on his angular jawline starkly contrast to the unhealthy pallor of his skin. His plump, deliciously shaped lips are still a faded, pale purple. At least his breathing is regular. The poor man must have been completely worn out to sleep for so many hours straight. As if the near drowning weren't enough, he's probably also sleep-deprived from his concert tour.

This man fast asleep in my condo is a famous performer. I can't imagine what it would be like to walk in Luca's shoes. To live that lifestyle. The glamour of the money and fame and crowds in awe of him come at the cost of a grueling schedule and being constantly hounded by the paparazzi.

No wonder he hides out in San Carlos. This quiet town has to be a wonderful break from the chaos of the big cities where he tours. In this community of mostly older Americans and Canadians—many of whom likely don't follow pop charts or have a clue who he is—he can go out without being recognized. He must relish the luxury of being anonymous.

I step back to my computer and open a file that contains the first chapter of my latest romance novel, *Forever by the Sea*. I write the scene where Arianna's dreaming—and where she has an erotic experience with a man she doesn't realize she's soon to meet in real life.

His lips crush against hers. The kiss grows, hotter, deeper, and more intense every second their lips and tongues collide. Arianna gasps with pleasure, desperate, wanting.

She grips his muscular shoulders tighter, digging her fingernails into his hard flesh. He's a carnal assault on her senses. His lips, his tongue, his hard body, which press against her closer, closer until she's pinned against the wall. His hand skims up her thigh, lifting the hem of her short dress until his fingers find her silk panties. Then they're inside her panties, sliding across her sensitive skin until one finger finds her wet slit. A shiver of delight runs through her. She spreads her legs wider, greedy for his touch.

I see Luca's face in front of my eyes as I write the scene. But now it's me there, rather than Arianna mashed up against the wall about to be penetrated. Hungry desire burns in his eyes as he touches me, stimulating my bud while I thrash and moan.

His tongue slides over his sensual lips and his gaze is riveted on my face as he sinks his finger inside my wet walls, thrusting in and out of me until the bursts of pleasure inside me intensify. I realize all at once that I'm grinding my pelvis against my chair, but I'm so lost in sensation that I'm on the edge of orgasm.

My finger drifts down and slides inside my panties. I stimulate my sensitive bud until my pleasure explodes and I ride the wave of ecstasy to its blissful end. Afterward, my body feels limp and my mind pleasantly hazy. I turn in my chair to make sure I haven't awakened Luca.

I wonder what would have happened if he had seen me touching myself. I can imagine the flare of hot desire in his eyes, how his dimples would deepen watching the erotic scene unfold.

His features would probably display that same primal need if he lined up his cock with my entrance and slowly sank inside, possessing me. That intense sexual undercurrent between us makes it nearly impossible to wipe these erotic images from my mind. At least all my libidinous daydreams liven up my writing.

Once I finish my word count for the day, I put on my headphones and listen to some of Luca's music on YouTube. I like every song I hear. His sensual, baritone voice seduced me the first time I heard it and excites me even more now that I know him. The accompanying instrumentals are a nice mix of jazz and pop. I download several songs to my iPad, including *"Mi Amor,"* the song that made me instantly crush on him during my drive down to Mexico.

My rumbling stomach reminds me it's dinner time. I head to the kitchen, wash my hands and then start washing and chopping vegetables. The kitchen is adjacent to the living room, with just a countertop of Mexican-tile separating the two rooms.

I decide to make extra food in case Luca stays for dinner. He should. He's in no shape to fix anything himself tonight. Too bad I don't have much in the fridge. Tomorrow's my normal shopping day. I don't even have a bottle of wine. At least I have some corn tortillas left. And a few Dos Equis. The food I usually fix is simple, healthy—the opposite of many Mexican-style foods that are fried and smothered with melted cheese and condiments. I do make good *chili rellenos,* though. Too bad I don't have all the ingredients to make those.

Now I'm fixing sea bass, sautéed in olive oil with onions, zucchini and tomatoes over rice. It's low in fat and high in nutrients and Omega 3s, which for me constitutes a perfect meal. Could be my healthy meal will be Luca's idea of the worst meal he's ever eaten in Mexico. Hopefully not.

"Something smells delicious."

I turn around to see Luca sitting up on the couch. He rubs his eyes and checks his watch. His eyes widen when he sees the time. "How could I sleep so long? It's nighttime already."

I study him, still stirring the food. "You almost drowned. And I bet you didn't sleep much last week either."

He rises from the couch, yawns, and stretches his arms in the air. He turns on the light on the side table. "No, I didn't." I'm still holding a spatula. My hand halts its stirring motions in the pan as I take him in. He looks way too good for the day he's endured. I'm happy to see some color has returned to his face. His curly hair is sticking out in random directions. Completely adorable.

He's removed the Mexican blanket I covered him with and now he's standing in my living room shirtless. Damn. He's got the best set of pecs, delts, and abs I've ever seen, that's for sure. And a five o'clock shadow on male magazine cover models doesn't usually make me salivate. But on Luca, the unkempt look is sheer hotness. He looks like what he'd look like…afterward. Oh, God, I shouldn't be thinking about that. Again. Like I was constantly today when writing my new novel.

Luca isn't some random guy I met at the beach. He's a star. Unobtainable. But the view. It's so hot. My gaze drifts toward the dark vee of hair that disappears into his swimsuit. My imagination starts undressing him. I tell myself, no, no, no. I can't go there. For the third time in the last hour.

I wonder how long I've been silent. Has he noticed how I've been staring? I clear my throat and stir the veggies vigorously. "Would you like a beer?"

"Oh, no, I really should be going."

"Why don't you stay awhile? You need to eat, and I've almost got dinner ready."

He walks into the kitchen bringing his hot body, sleep-swollen eyes and messy hair along with him. Damn, the man's distracting. His nearness sets all my nerve endings on fire. A thrill races up my spine. "Are you sure you want me to stay? I have been too much trouble for you already."

I turn toward him. "You're no trouble at all. Now how about that beer?"

He flashes his smile to great affect. His teeth are so straight and white, he could star in toothpaste commercials on the side. "Okay, I'll stay. You are very persuasive."

He's so close. Too close for me to be able to think straight. I struggle to remember what I just offered him. Oh, right, a beer. I pour a bottle of Dos Equis into a chilled glass from the freezer. "Here you go."

"Aren't you going to have one?"

"In a minute." I step back to the stove to stir the fish and vegetables.

"Here. You're busy. Let me get one for you." He pours beer into a second chilled glass and hands it to me.

"Thank you, Luca."

"My pleasure." He takes a big swallow of beer. Foam bubbles outline his upper lip. "I feel much more like myself now. Thank you for taking care of me."

He looks cute with those beer bubbles on his lips. I glance at his mouth, already imagining kissing those lips and tasting the beer froth and feeling the pressure of his mouth on mine. I take a long swallow of beer. "I'm glad I was able to help. That was a scary situation. It was lucky things turned out okay."

"You're being too nice. You mention scary, but what you don't say is what an idiot I was. I was swimming for almost an hour. I had this grand plan to show off my new and improved swimming skills for you. And my plan did not work out very well."

"You were out there for an hour?" I burst out laughing and instantly regret it. I press my lips together and shoot him a guilty look. "I'm sorry,

I shouldn't laugh. It's not really funny. But because you're okay, I can't help but laugh at the absurdity of it all. Men do such crazy things. I will never get it."

Luca frowns, then shakes his head. "You're right. Swimming so long in that heat was crazy. I was swimming after you because I knew you were upset, but I didn't see you and ended up further down the beach than I'd planned. And by the time I got back, I realized I was completely exhausted. Then I saw that guy touching you. When I started to sink, I kept thinking how wrong he was for you and how I wanted to be the one with your attention."

"Oh, Luca, I can't believe you thought I was interested in Justin. What a creep. He stood there laughing while you were out there fighting to stay afloat."

His lips curve up in a smile. His eyes flash a bright shade of green. "At least I got your attention."

I glance at him briefly and look away. His smooth talking and cute looks make it hard to stay upset with him. But they don't change the fact that he lied to me. I am not quite ready to let it go. "Yes, Luca, you did."

Satisfied that the food's done, I turn off the burner and set down the spatula. Then I open the cupboard and get two plates and place them on the countertop. I take two sets of silverware into the dining room and put them on the table.

Luca steps up beside me with a mischievous grin on his face. "At least I'm alive. And we're talking to each other. If I hadn't almost drowned, you might still be mad at me."

I plant my hands on my hips and stare at him. "How do you know I'm not still mad?"

"You kissed me down on the beach."

I frown and let out a long sigh. I flash back to that moment he was unconscious in the sand. The thought of him being hurt or worse struck the worst kind of fear in me. I kissed him because I was so happy to see he was okay. "Yes, I did. And you're right. I'm not mad anymore. But I do feel a bit overwhelmed."

Luca turns me toward him and places his hands on my shoulders. "I'm sorry, Jade. I never meant to cause you so much distress."

His touch is comforting, but if I don't keep my emotions in check, I'll fall in his arms and cry. I step slowly away. "I know. Dinner is ready now, Luca. Plates are here so you can serve yourself what you want. Hopefully, you can bear my American cooking."

"Your cooking woke me from a sound sleep, Jade. I'm sure it will be delicious." He picks up a plate and serves himself a generous amount of food. I wait until he finishes and then serve myself and follow him into the dining room. We sit directly across from each other.

His mouth closes over a forkful of fish. He chews the bite and when he finishes, he smiles and says, "This is delicious."

I can't help smiling. He eats quickly, which suggests he likes the food, but his manners indicate his mom taught him well. His napkin is neatly folded in his lap and he holds his fork the proper way, with his index finger resting on its back. He only puts small bites into his mouth, his jaw muscles working as he chews quietly and deliberately.

Within minutes he's cleaned his plate and is serving himself seconds. Either he's really starving and would eat cardboard if he had to, or he actually likes this meal. Hopefully, it's the latter. I wouldn't want to have to fix heavy meals for someone all the time. I don't like food with tons of grease and starch.

I reprimand myself for the thought. I've only made Luca this one dinner. And only because he was too worn out to go back to his condo and cook his own meal. I don't even know if he'll ever ask me out again.

"You seem distracted," says Luca. "What's on your mind?"

"Nothing important. I was just thinking this meal might not be what you're used to, that's all."

"Yes, and that's a very good thing. This meal is much better than the fast food meals we eat on tour. I've never been much for the American concept of food on the go. I only do eat fast food if I have to. Why rush through a meal or eat in the car when you can savor the food and enjoy long conversations with people you care about?

I nod and give him a smile. Relaxed meals are one of many things I love about Mexico. "I couldn't agree more. I've always liked real food.

Fast food tastes nasty and isn't healthy for you anyway. And good food with good company is what I like the best." When I say that, I think how much I want there to be more nights when I fix meals for Luca and I'm sitting across from him at this table.

"This food is light and nutritious and full of flavor."

"Thank you, Luca. I'm glad you like it."

He pauses for a moment and clears his throat. "After today, I'd understand it if you said *no*." His jaw clenches for just a moment before his facial features relax. Just when I think he's going to finish, there's a long hesitation. Or maybe it just seems like forever because I'm desperate to hear what he's about to say.

He's going to ask me out again. At least I hope. I want to burst out, *yes*, I want to go out with you again, but I don't want to look desperate. Or ridiculous. For all I know he's about to ask to borrow some eggs to make breakfast tomorrow. I rub my palms together under the table while I wait for him to continue.

"I wondered if you'd like to take a dinner cruise with me. I know someone here who owns a yacht. We could eat on the deck and watch the sunset. It could be nice."

"That sounds like a blast. I would love to go." I practically bounce out of my chair with excitement. So much for keeping my cool.

"Let me call my friend to see what nights are available. I'll let you know once I find out."

"Anytime this week is good for me."

He pushes his chair back. "I really should be going."

"Wait, before you go. I've been wanting to ask you something."

He gives me a curious smile. "And what's that?"

"I want to know what inspired you to become a singer. While you were sleeping, I looked you up online and listened to some of your YouTube videos."

His head lowers just enough that I notice. I think I see a flicker of sadness in his eyes. "Wait, I need for you to understand what I'm saying. I researched you online because I wanted to know more about you."

A faint smile raises the corner of his lips. "And what did you find out?"

I lean in toward him and rest one arm on the table, meeting his gaze. I tell him how I heard one of his songs on the radio during my drive to Mexico and how it grabbed me right away. "It moved me so much, it made me wish I understood enough Spanish to figure out the title. Only when I did the search a little while ago did I realize you were the singer. And then I couldn't wait to listen to all your songs. And I wasn't disappointed. Every one of them is full of meaning and depth. I cried, I laughed, I felt connected to the lyrics and the emotions I saw on your face when you performed."

He reaches for my hand and takes it gently in his. He gives it a squeeze before our hands land gently on the table. "Jade, you're such a wonderful surprise."

I laugh. "Why is that?"

"You teach swimming. You swim with dolphins. You're creative. Your gifts as a writer help you both appreciate and understand my music. You fascinate me."

I'm so unaccustomed to receiving compliments, I'm not sure how to respond. "That's good, I guess."

"It means a lot to me that you took the time to look me up and listen to my music. And hearing that it has meaning to you—that's what every artist wants to hear. I'm sure you like hearing that about your writing."

"Oh, definitely. I want my writing to touch people, to make a difference in their lives."

"Yes. That's what I want whenever I perform. Oh—and I can't wait to read one of your books."

"You don't have to. You probably wouldn't like them anyway. They're written for women." Heat rushes to my face as I imagine him reading the scene I wrote earlier.

"That doesn't matter. I want to read your work, Jade. You now know how I express my deepest feelings through my music—feelings that are universal and that many people connect to. I want to experience the art you've shared with the world."

"I'm flattered. But I'm no big-name author. I don't sell all that many books."

"Maybe you would if more people knew about them. It takes luck and being in the right place at the right time for an artist to succeed today. I'll read some of your books. And if you want, I'll help you make some connections."

"Luca, that's very thoughtful. But you don't have to do that. Being with you is what I want. I don't need you to do anything for me."

"Jade, I want to do things for you. You've taught me to swim, you saved my life, and you listened to my music. Oh, and served me that amazing meal. Please let me have a turn."

He speaks to me like an equal. A friend. Or maybe even a boyfriend. Which is hard to me to grasp because I'm still kind of intimidated by who he is. I keep asking myself the question, why me? "Okay. I'll let you try to help me."

"Good. Please tell me more about what you write."

"I write romance novels and do freelance content writing and editing."

"Romance novels? How interesting." His voice has a sensual edge to it. Our gazes lock and his stare heats my skin.

No man's ever excited me like this before. And he's not even touching me!

"How did you choose to write about love?"

"I got hooked on historical romances when I was a teen. I started writing romances and mysteries when I was in high school, but never finished any of them. My parents went ballistic when they found out I was writing so much. They said I'd end up homeless and begging on a street corner."

Luca's jaw clenches and his skin darkens. His voice rings with protective anger. "That's ridiculous. I hope you didn't listen to that nonsense."

It moves me to see how upset he is at hearing how my parents tried to stop me from doing what made me happy. "My father said he wouldn't pay for me to go to college unless I studied something he thought made sense. I majored in structural engineering at the University of Arizona."

"Engineering is so rigid. I can't picture you working in that field."

"The coursework was total drudgery. The only good thing was that I managed to squeeze a few creative writing electives in. After I graduated, an engineering firm in Tucson hired me. I worked there for seven years."

"When did you start writing full-time?"

"I wrote on the side from the beginning, then quit my job last year when my writing work started paying enough for me to get by."

He must have heard the ring of sadness in my voice because he reaches out and brushes his hand over my arm. "Wait. There's more to this story that you're not telling me. I can see by your expression." His voice sounds so compassionate and kind, I nearly burst into tears.

It's validating to have my dream understood. When I made the choice that gave me so much joy, I wanted to jump and shout, but I didn't hear a word of congratulations from Kelsi or Brandon, only harsh words and reprimands. "I made the right choice. I've been much happier working as a writer. But the news didn't sit well with my boyfriend. Or my sister."

He's clenching his jaw again. I can tell because his dimples just got deeper. "Why didn't they want you to do what was best for you?"

"I don't know. I guess they just don't get me."

"I understand that, believe me. Many people can be blind to things they don't wish to see."

"I know, right? But how did you manage to swing this conversation over to me? Just a minute ago, we were talking about your music career."

"It just happened. Maybe because you're much more fascinating." A yellowish-green flicker of desire appears in his eyes. His gaze wanders toward my breasts and back to my face again.

Warmth spreads through my belly. Luca knows how to make me feel like a woman. That look of want in his eyes makes my body vibrate with need. And at the same time every word he says feels like a gentle caress. His words are such a comfort. Admiration isn't something I hear too often when someone learns I'm a writer. Usually, they wrinkle their noses like they smell something bad. Or ask me if I've ever had a *real job*. "I don't know about that. But there's something I've been wanting to ask you about your work."

"What's that?"

"What moves you to create?"

He doesn't speak right away. But a soft expression washes over his features, making him look almost boyish. "Many things move me. My love for my country moves me. The love for my mother moves me." He studies me for a moment, his blue-green eyes shining with an intensity I haven't seen before. "You move me."

My whole body feels like it's going to melt when he says those words. "Luca," I whisper.

"It's true, Jade. That first morning when I saw you swimming out there in the sea, I couldn't look away. I watched the rhythm of your stroke. How the dolphins came near you. I'd only seen you from a distance when words to a song popped into my head."

A song. About me? Cozy warmth envelopes me. I can hardly catch my breath. "You wrote a song about me?" This is so romantic. Like something straight from a dream.

But it's really happening. The famous Luca Espinoza is sitting beside me—looking incredibly gorgeous—and just told me that what I love most—swimming in the sea—moved him enough to write a song about me. It's unbelievable.

But he moved me, too. I felt like a tremor moved the earth when we met. My creativity has surged since then. Lines of dialogue spontaneously pop into my head. While I'm swimming. Even when I wake up at night. And I have to rush to the computer to type it all into my manuscript. I met Luca and the words just seemed to flow. I captured many of the universal feelings women experience when they fall for a guy—the sexual attraction, the obsession, the angst over waiting for a call, the wondering what is going on in his mind.

And the writing helped me cope with the emotional rollercoaster I've been on lately. I finished writing one book and published it and am already working on another one when I usually need two or three weeks to recharge first.

He fuels my creative fire. But there are other fires he's stoked. Fires of attraction and desire.

"Yes, it's called 'Jade's song.'"

"No way. You named it after me?"

"Of course. It's about you. Don't look so surprised. You're a fascinating woman, Jade. I don't know why you can't see that."

"I don't know. I feel... ordinary. I've never thought of myself as the kind of person anyone would want to write songs about."

"Maybe you need to see yourself the way I see you instead of the way your family saw you."

I pause and study his face, wondering what he does see when he looks at me. When I look in the mirror, I see a woman barely getting by on a writer's meager earnings. I see a woman men only want for short-term enjoyment. A woman eventually slated to be tossed away, the way Brandon discarded me.

I see a woman who could never please her parents. Who looks plain and ordinary compared to her drop-dead gorgeous sister. I see a woman, unlike Kelsi, who couldn't stick with most people's idea of a suitable career.

My parents gushed all over the place when Kelsi told them she wanted to be a plastic surgeon. "Your sister has direction in life," my mom said one day, when she found me in my room writing another novel. "You should stop wasting your time writing that gibberish and start researching remunerative careers."

I feel talented and interesting and worthwhile while I'm out in the sea swimming. The sea reassures me. It says I'm fine right now, the way I already am. That I don't have to change to please anyone. Sometimes, though, when I'm out of my element, it's hard to believe.

Luca leans in closer. "You seem sad. What's the matter?" I look up from the table to meet his gaze.

"I keep thinking about things people have said to me over the years. That I need to change, that I'm not good enough. It's hard to sort it all out."

"You need to let it all go. Don't you see how wrong they were?"

"I want to."

"They were blind. I have the same eyes that you do. The eyes of an artist. And I see you as the most amazing woman, Jade. A woman with so much talent and a gift that few people on earth have—not only that you are such a strong swimmer, but that you have nurtured that talent so that it brings you peace. You have done what many others could never do—earn the confidence of the dolphins. They connect with you. Most people would be afraid to get that close to them."

I remember how Justin said I was stupid to swim with dolphins, how they would hurt me. People like him say things to me and I start to doubt myself. I've been doing this ever since I was little. Letting what other people think sink in too deep. I let their thoughts matter more than my own. But I don't know how to not do it.

"I'm sorry, Jade. I can tell I've upset you."

"No, it's not that. You say the most wonderful things, Luca. I keep thinking about all the bad stuff people have said to me. I need to learn to shut it down instead of letting it affect me so much."

"Yes, you do," he agrees.

"But sometimes it's hard to get all that out of my head." Then I tell Luca what Justin said to me about the dolphins.

He shakes his head and runs a thumb over the prickly shadow on his jaw. "Nothing that guy says is worth listening to."

I laugh. "I know. He's a complete jerk."

"Justin. Your sister. Your parents. Whatever-his-name-was, the ex-boyfriend who was not worthy of you. They all have one thing in common."

"What's that?"

"They only see what they think you should be, not who you really are. You can never be happy if you try to please people like that."

"I know that's true. Since I met you, not only have I been writing more, but I haven't been thinking as much about Ja—" I cover my mouth with one hand. I've said too much. I shouldn't open up so much. It makes me too vulnerable. Luca probably has a different girlfriend every month. He has to know what women want to hear. What if he doesn't mean what he says? What if all this smooth talk is just to get me into bed?

"I see that look in your eyes. Jade? Please. Tell me."

"I like you, Luca. More than you even know. But I'm afraid. I don't want to get hurt again."

Luca stands up and walks behind to my chair. He drapes his hands over my shoulders and leans in close to my ear. "I will be good to you, Jade, I promise. I want to do things for you. That's all I've thought about since I left here a week ago."

His words sound sincere. But I can't wrap my brain around all this. Why would this gorgeous, famous, wealthy guy who can have anyone want to be with me? I'm attractive, sure, but no one would call me beautiful. I'm not exceptional. "There are thousands of women like me in the world. And you could have anyone. It doesn't make sense."

He reaches for my upper arms and lifts me from the chair. He turns me around to face him. "You write about love, don't you?"

"Yes." I see the Sea of Cortez and emotions I've always dreamed of seeing in a man's eyes. I see compassion and understanding. His thoughts are here with me and not drifting off to whatever or whoever is next on his to-do list.

"Does love always make sense? Does a person just get up one morning and say I'm going to fall for someone today?" He skims a finger ever so slowly over my cheek.

"No, most of the time there's no logic to it. It just happens."

"Yes. And as for what you said about thousands of women. It's not like that, Jade. I've met many women. None of them are like you. For some reason, you judge yourself too harshly, you allow the words of people who don't understand you to burrow into your brain. How many people can swim like you? How many people have that confidence to go out in the sea—an alien environment—and try to find peace there? How many people would have been brave enough to swim out and save a drowning man the way you did today? How many, Jade?"

Tears flood my eyes and roll down my cheeks. "I don't know. Not many, I guess." My life feels perfect whenever I'm out in the sea. Then when I'm back on land, the negative thoughts worm their way back in. What if I stopped listening to those thoughts? That's what I came here to do after all. To start over and be free. To truly begin living my life the way I want to. Until I can get my thoughts under control, I won't truly be free.

Luca's voice is gentle, his breath tickling my ear. "You are special, Jade. Watching you swim made me want to know what it was like to be out in the sea surrounded by those dolphins. The way you swim looks so smoothed and relaxed, you looked like you belonged with them." He squeezes my shoulder and then returns to his chair.

He's spot on. The dolphins know I'm different, but they don't have any problem with it. I feel more connected to them than I do with most people. I felt disconnected from everyone until I came down here. But now things are changing. For the first time, I know some of my neighbors. I met Gabriela and Martin and they treat me like family. And now there's Luca. "You really wanted to be out there? I figured you just said that to start a conversation. That's why I offered to teach you to swim. Because I wanted to see if you were serious."

"Testing me, were you?" He leans in and nudges me with one shoulder and I laugh.

"Maybe."

"Did I pass?"

"During the lessons, yes. Today, not so much."

His face darkens. Even his eyes darken to a bluish shade of gray, like the sea when a cloud passes over it. "I wish I could forget about my terrible mistake. But I meant what I said about wanting to learn to swim and wanting to feel connected to nature. I have felt that connection a few times before when I've been here in San Carlos. I like to watch the sky burst with color after a sunset and the pelicans gliding over the waves and gulls squawking over a stolen meal. But when you took me out to meet the dolphins. Jade, I'll never forget that. And your dolphin friends came to rescue me."

Luca surprises me. What sounds like something a guy would say to get me to sleep with him ends up being the truth. There's a bond between us that's very special. It makes me realize more than ever that Brandon and I had nothing in common. We were like oil and water.

Luca and I have everything—off-the-charts attraction, deep conversation, and a way of being with each other that's easy, dare I say it, even cozy. I could get used to this—which both excites and scares me. So many nights I've eaten dinner here alone, then curled up in the living room chair to read a book. I always enjoyed it before. But this evening with Luca is even better. I enjoy the companionship. "I'm glad you enjoyed it, Luca. I'm glad I could teach you swim. I hope what happened today won't keep you out of the water. If you're wise, you can be safe."

He frowns and drops his gaze for a moment before looking back up at me. "I'm anxious about it. But I want to get back in the water right away. I can't let fear win."

He looks so serious, I smile and joke with him to lift some of his worry. "If you don't mind, we'll wait until morning. I'm not much into night swimming."

His laugh and the flash of his smile is a pleasant reward. "I know you're joking, but I can tell you right now, you'll never get me to swim in the dark."

"You never know." My words come out sounding more flirtatious than I intended. Perhaps because I'm envisioning our naked bodies entangled in the sighing sea under the starlight. "But we'll go in the water in the morning. Just for a few minutes And I'll be right there with you." I long to comfort him the way he has been comforting me.

"*Gracias,* Jade. I would like that." Just hearing his soothing voice and seeing his kind eyes and the soft tip of his brows makes me wish he would never leave. But he pushes his chair back and stands up. "I really must be going. I rise and prepare to walk him to the door. But he takes a step closer and leans in toward me. The dark hint of sex burns in his eyes.

My heart races faster. Every molecule in my body vibrates with excitement. His mouth is only inches away and closing. He's going to kiss me. With those sexy, swollen lips. With those lips I've thought of constantly since our post-dinner-date kiss. That night, the meeting of our mouths ended much too quickly.

His lips come closer, and hover over mine. He smells like salty sea and sweat. His mouth brushes softly over mine. That first contact sends shivers cascading all the way down to my toes. He nibbles on my lower lip. I reciprocate before instinct takes over. I no longer have to think about what to do next. My mouth eagerly devours his. Our kiss feels right. I don't want it to be over in an instant. I want it to last all night.

His hands skim up my back, slowly, seductively, stoking my desire. I told myself I didn't want to get involved. And I didn't want another man like Brandon. But I want Luca. I ache for him. As we continue to kiss, breathless, desperate, hot, his hands grip the back of my head, pulling me closer so our lips—our bodies—are smashed together.

His perfect mouth—this one I've dreamed of constantly since our first date—is once again mine. He nibbles my lower lip again and then slides his tongue over the seam of my mouth. I sigh with pleasure and open my lips to give him entrance. His tongue greedily penetrates my mouth in a hot and demanding way that sends a rush of aching heat between my thighs. Every cell in my body vibrates with need.

His hands skim down the length of my spine, igniting a trail of heat. He grips me tighter, compressing my breasts against his tightly muscled chest. The sudden, searing contact of our bodies sends hot blood rushing south. His firm thighs press against my pelvis. When his arousal swells against my inner thighs, the pulsing ache between my thighs intensifies. The closer we get, the more I want him. The more I need him. And I want and need Luca desperately. Urgently. I'll lose my mind if I don't give in to my desire.

I pull him in closer—digging my nails into his back as our mouths move against each other, wet, hot, exploring. A strap on my sundress slides down my shoulder. He pushes it down further until one of my breasts is exposed. I gasp when he palms my breast in his hand, massaging, teasing, until I pant with lust.

My fast-beating pulse and our heavy breathing slowly overrides the sounds of the waves and music at the beach coming through the open windows as I see, taste and experience Luca. Every part of me wants Luca naked and inside me.

He slides the other strap off my shoulder, exposing the second breast. A shiver of delight races through me. Most of my torso is now exposed. He kisses his way down my neck, searing a trail over my skin until his lips reach my breast. I shouldn't let him do this, I think faintly. It's too dangerous. I'll end up getting hurt.

He brings the nipple to a peak with his tongue. My head falls back in a groan and my mind empties. Each flick of his tongue sends shockwaves of pleasure through my body. My panties feel drenched, I'm so turned on. My body trembles with need.

One of Luca's hands strokes my cheek. "I don't want to scare you."

"You're not," I protest, but my words sound lame even to my own ears.

He studies me. His blue-green eyes miss nothing, see much more than the expression on my face. They see deep inside me. "You're not fine, Jade. I can tell. Let's not do this. Not until you're ready to trust me."

I bury my face in his chest, feeling embarrassed. And let down. I wanted him to make love to me, even though I was afraid. Maybe he won't want me anymore now that he knows how insecure I am.

"I can see by the look on your face that doubting thoughts are running through your mind. Please, just relax. Let's sit down and get to know each other." He slides my dress back up over my breasts, gently settling the straps where they belong on my shoulders.

"I'm sorry," I say, looking down, unable to meet his gaze. "I didn't mean to spoil everything."

He lifts my chin gently and leans in closer. "Please don't apologize. You did nothing wrong. It wasn't the right time, that's all. There is no hurry. We have plenty of time." His voice is so deep and controlled and gentle. As if the sudden end to that smoldering kiss didn't faze him at all.

"You're not upset with me?"

"No, of course not." He takes my hand. "Come over to the couch and sit with me." He tugs me toward it and I follow, dropping down beside him on the cushions.

I can't look him in the eyes. "Before I met you, I had made up my mind to stay away from men."

"Is it because of what happened with your boyfriend?"

"Yes, mostly. He made me feel insignificant and disposable."

"That's because he was a jerk. You deserve much better, Jade."

I exhale. "Looking back on it, I think I settled for what I thought I deserved. Which wasn't much. There were signs all along that our relationship wasn't working, but I guess I ignored them. I thought he was going to ask me to marry him that night he took me out for a special dinner and ended up dumping me. The next thing I knew, he was telling me there was someone else and that it was over between us."

Luca's fists tighten and the dimples around his lips deepen. "The more you tell me about him, the more I hate this guy. How could he be so insensitive?"

It moves me how protective he is of me, how it bothers him so much that I've been hurt. "I don't know. I'll never understand it. But I appreciate that you understand how hard it was for me."

"Of course, I do. I would have punched the guy if I'd been in that restaurant."

I burst out laughing. Luca's kind words are like an ointment for my pain—they soothe it all away. "That would have made the evening much better, that's for sure."

Luca reaches for my hand again, weaving his fingers through mine. He shifts our joined hands in his direction and sets them softly in his lap. His gaze is compassionate, the expression on his face sad. "I'm sorry he caused you so much pain. You didn't deserve that."

"I wish he could have just been honest. He could have mentioned months earlier that the relationship wasn't working out for him. But I never knew this was going on in his mind. When he just dumped me out of the blue like that, I felt like such an idiot for not seeing the writing on the wall. But maybe, I didn't want to see it."

"Jade, you shouldn't blame yourself. He deceived you."

I sigh. "I know."

"He made the mistake. There is no relationship without honesty."

"But I still feel like such a fool."

"It wasn't your fault. You should be able to trust someone close to you. Instead he betrayed your trust."

I remember all the sleepless nights I tossed and turned in bed, thinking about what I could have done differently, trying to guess what I had done wrong.

"Please, Jade. I know what you're thinking. I don't understand it, but I know. You're doubting yourself again. Please don't. He was the one that was unworthy. Not you. You're an amazing woman. You shouldn't ever let anyone convince you you're anything less. You don't need to change for anyone. He didn't deserve you. You deserve someone who will take cherish you, and not treat you callously."

Everything he says makes sense. "I know you're right. And talking to you about this makes me feel better. But sometimes doubts creep in. I suppose that's why I'm afraid to trust anyone."

"I understand. It's going to take some time."

"Doesn't it bother you that I'm such a basket case?"

"No. You've been hurt, and you need time to heal. I will show you I am worthy of your trust. It will be a challenge. But it is one I am up to."

He's not at all like American men. For one, he has that Mexican-Italian accent and roll to his *r*s that sends a sexy thrill down my spine. But it's much more than that. He doesn't keep his emotions so closely guarded. He shares his deepest thoughts with me. He's considerate and caring. And he's patient instead of seeming desperate to get me in bed. "I appreciate that, Luca. I really do. But now that I know about your glamorous career, I'm more scared than ever about being with you. Women must throw themselves at you all the time."

"Yes, women chase me. But I'm not interested in any of them. I find them more of a nuisance than anything else. I have needs, like any other man. I have had the occasional quick involvement, but nothing lasting. I know what I want in a woman, Jade, and I can honestly say that those groupies do not even come close to what I'm looking for."

Imagining Luca having sex with another woman else hurts, but visualizing him married sends pinpricks of pain shooting through my chest. I want to envision me at his side. But I keep seeing him with a voluptuous Mexican woman with a waterfall of dark hair and smooth, golden skin. She'd be at home caring for their four children while he traveled the globe, performing. I fight back tears. I shouldn't be thinking like this. I barely even know Luca. Falling for him so fast is unwise. "And what is that?"

"That answer is easy—especially when I look at you. I want to be with a woman who is intelligent and interesting, a woman who is open and honest and whose company I enjoy so much I know I will never tire of talking to her. I want to be with a woman who loves me—not for my fame or money—but because I'm the man she wants."

Is he really saying what I think he's saying? That he's found the woman he wants—and it's me? "Wow."

"I hope what I said doesn't upset you, Jade. What I'm saying is one-hundred percent the truth. I see us together for a long time. I told you this because you need to know, and I want you to stop doubting yourself. Not to put pressure on you. We can take it slow. Take things one day at a time."

"But you'll be gone again soon. Won't you want someone else?"

"No, Jade. I only want you."

He gazes at me with intensity blazing in his eyes, like he means what he says. If only it weren't so hard for me to accept. When I'm with him, I can absolutely believe every word. But will I when he's gone?

He flashes me a boyish smile and lifts his hands from his lap and sweeps them through the air like he's conducting and orchestra. "I have an idea. Why don't you come with me on my next tour? I'm going to Germany and Austria in two weeks."

I cross my arms over my chest and lean back against the cushions. Images of my face popping up online and in gossip rags flash in front of my eyes. Being with Luca will be about as far from low profile as I can get. People will find out who I am and rip me to shreds. They'll post photos of me looking stressed out or wearing clothes that make me look fat, and say I'm not good enough for him. "Oh, no, I couldn't."

"Why not? The hotels will be very comfortable. While I'm practicing, you will have plenty of downtime to do your writing. I can even extend our stay so we'll have time to enjoy ourselves. I can get you a stage pass, too, for as many performances as you would like to attend."

I shouldn't let fear get in the way. His plan does sound incredible. I've always wanted to go to Europe, but Brandon never wanted to go. And now I finally have the chance and I'd get to go with Luca. We have so much fun together. I'm starting to fall for him, big time.

But what if I'm halfway around the world and all of a sudden he decides I'm not right for him? I'll be thousands of miles away from San Carlos—the place I now feel safe. And I'll be more alone than ever. "I—uh, don't know. It does sound like the chance of a lifetime."

Luca's smiling now. And his eyes flash with excitement. He knows he's half-convinced me to go along with his plan. "Austria's beautiful this time of year. Flowers in the meadows, snow in the mountains, everything green and lush and summery."

Luca knows how to be persuasive. But I'm anxious. Taking this risk seems, well, risky. "It sounds like a dream."

"Then say yes to that dream. Say yes to an escape with me."

"But you'll be too busy to have me tagging along, won't you?" If I can talk myself out of this, I will.

"All the concerts are at night. I'll have time every day to spend with you. And we'll go early and stay a couple of days afterward."

I wonder how much the plane ticket will cost. It's not in my budget to spend a bunch of money on travel, but there's no way I'm going to ask him to pay my way. I can make the money up somehow. I'll just pare my expenses to the bone for a few months afterward.

"I can see it in your eyes. Your mind is busy again."

"Okay, I'll go. Maybe later you can text me the itinerary you want me to book."

"That won't be necessary, Jade. We will be flying via private jet. I just need to change the dates. You don't have to worry about anything."

"I need to help cover the costs."

Luca's brows tip inward. "No, Jade, you don't," he says firmly.

I shake my head. "Oh, no, that wouldn't be right. I need to pay my fair share."

"Please, Jade. Let me do this for you. I can tell you want to go on the trip. Just say yes and let me take care of the rest. I could never spend all the money I make, so let me spend some of it on you. We'll have a great time, you'll see."

How can I say no? He wants me to go to Europe with him. My heart beats faster. I squirm on the couch, unable to sit still. The trip sounds exciting and fun. "Okay, I'll go."

CHAPTER TWENTY-ONE

Jade

"This is unbelievable." Luca and I walk across the tarmac, holding hands, ready to board the slender white private jet.

He smiles at me. He's dressed casually today—in jeans that hug his butt and a gray button-up shirt stretched tight by his broad shoulders and muscular chest. As always, he looks good enough to eat. "Trust me, this is the only way to fly. You won't have to choke down stale peanuts or be squeezed into only seventy-five centimeters of leg room."

"Thank goodness for that."

"Go ahead." Luca gestures for me to go first up the steps onto the plane he told me earlier is a Gulfstream G550. I feel his supportive touch on my back as he follows me.

I gasp when I see the plane's interior. It looks more like the inside of a house than any airplane I've ever seen. "This is awesome." I notice a few people are already seated. They must be the members of Luca's band.

"Our seats are in front. I'll introduce you to the guys here in a minute."

I walk across the hardwood floors, admiring the rows of comfy looking tan leather seats with tables. There's even an enormous leather couch with plump pillows perched at either end. Large round windows offer a clear view of the outside.

We'll probably have a to-die-for view of the Sea of Cortez from the air.

I've only flown three times before and never in first class, let alone on a private jet. And now I'm about to fly to Europe in luxurious comfort. Before we settle into our seats, Luca introduces me to his band.

He told me earlier that the plane would be stopping at various airports to pick up his band members from various places they'd been spending their vacations before flying her to Guaymas to pick us up.

I exchange a kiss on the cheek first with Luca's brother, Lorenzo, who plays the saxophone, before greeting Raphael, the trombone player, and Steve and Larry, the two percussionists. We engage in a few minutes of small talk. I like them all right away. They seem friendly and easy going and none of them asks me any prying questions.

"Let's go find our seats," Luca suggests. We walk toward the front of the plane. "Why don't you take the window seat. You'll like the view."

"I'm sure."

He places his hand on my shoulder and waits for me to sit down before he takes the seat beside me. "You'll find a bin under the seat where you can stow your backpack and purse."

The plush leather seat molds to my hips and back. This is so cool. I can't believe I'm sitting on this amazing plane with this drop-dead gorgeous, famous guy who is sort-of my boyfriend. Wow. Just wow. I squirm with excitement in my seat.

I retrieve what I need from my backpack and purse before tucking them away in the bin under the seat. Luca shows me another compartment for newspapers and electronic devices and how my chair fully reclines at the push of a button for sleep.

"Are you comfortable?" Luca reaches for my hand. Our fingers interlace, and he gives my hand a squeeze. He looks so hot today – the three top buttons undone on his shirt show off a delicious swath of his chest that is all hard muscle. I know. Because I've smoothed my hands over the solid contours of his chest. Every ridge is sculpted of well-trained muscle. He hasn't allowed his grueling travel schedule to get in the way of working out.

He looks like he's never missed a day of training. Or ever indulged in too many desserts or too many drinks. Just looking at him is more of an indulgence than a chocolate truffle or an ice-cold daquiri. I'll never get over the fact that Luca's so damn good looking. And that he's chosen me.

"Comfortable. Are you kidding? Everything about this plane is incredible."

He smiles, showing a flash of white teeth, which contrast against his olive skin. "I'm glad you like it. The experience is going to get even better. Soon, Veronica will be making the rounds serving champagne."

I laugh, feeling happy and carefree. "Champagne? Really? That's pretty awesome."

Moments later, Veronica steps out from what looks like a private room in the front of the plane. She introduces herself and then hands us glasses of bubbly in etched crystal flutes. "Please let me know if you need anything during the flight, Miss," she says.

"We will, Veronica. Thank you." Luca raises his glass in the air.

Our gazes connect as our glasses clink together. "To our European trip," he says. And I return the greeting. The toast is just for the two of us. We sip from our glasses. I can hear Luca's band members talking and laughing somewhere behind us. Obviously, they're all enjoying themselves, too.

How could anyone not have a blast traveling like this. It's crazy. I'm used to resigning myself to hours of hell and misery whenever I board a plane. "Oh, Luca, I'm so excited to be taking this trip with you."

"I'm glad, Jade. I want you to have a good time."

I take another sip of the dry champagne. The bubbles tickle my throat and my nose. A giddy laugh escapes my lips. This feels unreal. Like a dream. Luca always makes me feel special. No man's ever made me feel this special before. He said we were right for each other. It scared me to hear it, mostly because I've been deceived before.

But something's happening to me. I can't deny it any more. I can't convince myself it's just a temporary obsession or a crush. I know now,

I'm falling in love with Luca. His gentle words, his compassion and understanding, his touch and the raging passion between us make me want to hang onto him and never let go.

He leans in and kisses me on the cheek. "I'm glad I get to be the one to show you Europe for the first time."

I meet his gaze and smile. "Going to places I've dreamed about visiting for years is amazing enough. But going with you is the best part." He kisses me again, this time softly on the lips.

He knows I meant what I said. He must know that he has latched onto my heart. This mind-blowing, luxurious lifestyle just happens to be an extra perk that comes along with the package. Not that I'm complaining about it. What girl wouldn't want to sit and drink champagne with a man like Luca on a private jet?

"I can't wait for you to see Salzburg. We'll have time to sightsee and adjust to the time zone change before we fly to Vienna for my first performance."

"I want to see that castle up on the hill you told me about earlier."

"We can go tomorrow if you like."

My voice almost comes out in a squeal. "Oh, I would love it."

Luca laughs, puts his arm around me and pulls me in closer. We keep on chatting about everything we'll do in Salzburg over a second glass of champagne. Our conversation is relaxed and easy, it's as if we've known each other forever.

"I took my mom on one of my tours last year. We went to Prague, Warsaw and Budapest."

"Did she enjoy it?"

"Oh, yes, very much. I took her up on stage and had her sit beside me while I performed a song I wrote the lyrics to that I dedicated to her."

"That must have meant a lot to her."

"I know it did. She cried when I sang that song. I came close to crying too. She means so much to me." His blue-green eyes shine with tears, but he blinks them away, and that trace of deep emotion I saw for just a moment is gone.

"I can tell, Luca. I wish I could have seen that."

His lips turn up in a grin. "You didn't find that one on YouTube?"

"No, not yet. But now I want to see it."

"One day I'll take you to meet my mother. I know she will like you."

"I would love to meet your mom." I feel my gut twist. What if Luca's mamá finds me inadequate the way my parents did? What would Luca's mother think about him dating someone like me—an American woman with no real family. She'd undoubtedly want to see Luca with a Catholic Mexican woman surrounded by doting relatives.

"What's wrong, Jade?" Luca asks.

"I was just thinking how your mother would probably be disappointed to see you with an American woman, especially given my family situation."

"Those things are only on the surface, Jade. My mother will see the depth in you. She always appreciates people with a kind heart. And if she sees that you are good for me, she will love you very much. Without question."

He's done it again. Said the right words. Smoothed away any doubts. He's the only person who's ever been able to do that. Before he came into my life, only swimming in the sea could make everything right.

Veronica appears with our dinner—on real china instead of plastic trays. My mouth waters at the sight of the food. My plate has a generous juicy slab of prime rib, along with diced potatoes and mixed vegetables. There's even a tossed salad with dressing in a tiny crystal cruet and crème brûlée.

"Would you like a dinner roll, Miss?" Veronica asks. She's holding an enormous basket of bread that smells like it came straight from the oven.

"Yes, please. That would be lovely." I smile and reach for one of the rolls. She hands me a small dish with two round scoops of butter.

Luca and I exchange more smiles than words while we eat our meal. I chew on a tender bite of meat, savoring the taste as it practically melts in my mouth. Each bite delivers a delicious burst of flavor to my taste buds.

I never thought of eating as sexy. But watching Luca eat turns me on. His full lips are slick with oil from the juicy meat. And the way he slides his tongue over his lips sometimes makes my nipples tighten. I imagine his tongue tasting my skin. I feel a rush of heat between my thighs. And I can tell by Luca's heavy-lidded gaze and the gold flash in his eyes, that he's feeling the heat as much as I am.

I scoop the last bite of crème brûlée from the crystal bowl and savor the sweet bite. Then I lick the last bit of sweetness from my lips.

"You missed a spot," says Luca seductively. He kisses me, gently biting my lip. "Mmm. Tastes good."

"You taste good too."

He pulls away when Veronica appears. She clears away our trays and disappears behind a closed door. The cabin lights slowly dim. The air feels chilly and I shiver.

"Are you cold?"

"Yes, a little."

Luca pulls a blanket out of the compartment under the seat. He unfolds it and stretches it over my legs and my lap. He covers most of his lower body, too. When he looks at me again, I see mischief dancing in his eyes. He positioned the blanket like that on purpose. I see his hand wandering toward me under the blanket. He meets my gaze as his hand finds my bare thigh and slowly skims up, pushing the hem of my dress higher and higher.

"Do you want me to stop?" he asks.

My face flushes hot. Luca's fingers haven't even wandered into my panties yet and I'm already feeling guilty. "No." My voice sounds breathless and desperate. The heat between us is so exciting. Imagining him touching me there on a plane like this, it feels forbidden. I burn with desire for his touch and know his masculine fingers will explore and tantalize all my sensitive places.

Luca presses a button on a remote control he's holding. "Let's give ourselves a little more privacy." Bunched up curtains I didn't notice before slide across a suspended wire, isolating us from the rest of the plane. Luca sets down the remote and leans in to possess my mouth again. His lips are hot and wet and taste sugary sweet. Our kiss deepens, becoming more and more primal as our mouths crush together, tasting, biting, devouring. Luca slides his tongue along the seam of my lips, teasing my mouth open. I eagerly accommodate him, allowing his tongue to penetrate my mouth. A frenzy of lust overpowers me. His tongue inside my mouth makes me ache for the sensation of his cock sinking deep inside me.

As our tongue war wages on, his hand rides back up my thigh. His fingers glide over my skin with erotic ease, working their way inside my panties. He slides a finger along the length of my slit. "Oh, you're wet," he says. I spread my legs wider to give him more access. He separates my nether lips and sinks a finger deep into my wetness.

I'm so turned on by the forbidden nature of what we're doing that I'm drenched. My mouth falls open and I moan with pleasure. Heat surges through my body like a high voltage electric current. Sex on an airplane never even crossed my mind. But this is no ordinary airplane. And Luca is no ordinary man. He smells and tastes so good and his touch is hot fuel scorching every nerve ending in my body. This is naughty. And exciting. I don't hear any voices. Maybe Luca's brother and the other band members have fallen asleep. But they're not that far away from us. The equivalent of maybe eight rows back on a commercial plane. They can't see us. The aircraft engine mutes most of the surrounding noises. But not all of them. Will they hear us? When his finger settles on my nub, I pant with lust. Do I even care?

One of his fingers stimulates my nub while another penetrates my opening. I can hear the slick sound of his finger moving in and out of me. The wanton sensation drives me wild. I buck and squirm and grind my hips in toward him as pleasure bursts through my core. He intensifies the pressure on my bud.

I feel a shift in the position of his fingers and look up to see Luca is no longer in his seat. He's dropped down onto the floor. His head dives between my legs as he pushes a button and slowly reclines my seat. I feel a gush of wet heat between my legs thinking about what he's going to do to me now, how good his tongue is going to feel on my vulnerable flesh. He gazes up at me, a roguish grin on his face. Then his tongue slides along the seam of my slit. A whimper escapes my lips as hot pleasure rips through me.

Sudden inhibition makes me lift my head and look at him. "What are you doing?" Why did I say that? Isn't it obvious? But I can't believe he's going down on me.

"I'm going to taste you until you go completely crazy." He licks me again.

I groan. From the pleasure and out of desperation for more of it. "I might lose control."

"I want to give you pleasure, Jade. Relax. *Por favor*."

His deep voice turns me on almost as much as the lusty flash of light I see in his blue-green eyes as he gazes between my wide spread legs and licks his lips. Is he fantasizing about fucking me? God, how my opening aches for him to fill me. I lay back on the seat and allow myself to forget my inhibitions. His tongue laps over me, stimulating my bud, sending hot blazes of pleasure shooting through my center. Then he plunges one finger inside, fucking me slowly and then more rapidly with his finger. I undulate against him. My brain slowly starts to overdose on sensation.

I gasp and pant and squirm with lust. He penetrates me with two fingers, stretching me wider. My walls contract around his fingers as my excitement builds. And builds. Until I feel like I'm about to burst from the pleasure. This feels so fucking good. A finger tortures and torments my clit again and then I explode, thrashing and bucking as my orgasm overtakes me.

After the waves of pleasure subside, I lay limp in my seat looking at him. I wonder if he would let me return the favor. But when he stands up and unzips his pants, I know he has something else in mind. The ache between my legs is almost painful. Even though he just made me come, his cock thrusting deep inside me is what I really want.

He tugs off his shirt and casts it aside. His pants drop to the floor and he kicks them out of the way. Seeing him naked on this plane is so erotic. Every inch of his perfect body is honed out of rock-hard, rippling muscle.

His cock stands tall and erect. Damn, he's big. My inner walls clench with anticipation. I'm still sprawled out in my seat, my dress hiked up over my hips, my silk panties pulled enough to the side to expose my opening. The forbidden nature of him preparing to fuck me when I'm dressed makes me wriggle on my seat with anticipation. His bicep muscles bunch as he rips open the foil package and slides a condom over his length. "I need to be inside you, Jade. I want to make love to you."

"Please, Luca. It's what I want, too." I'm lying on my back, exposed and vulnerable. Another jolt of heat surges between my thighs when he pulls the thin strip of silk over from my opening and lines his cock up at my entrance. My pussy tightens. He's going to fuck me. Right here on this plane. And I'm so ready for it, I spread my legs open wider, desperate for his entry.

He crouches over me straddling the seat, sinking a teasing inch inside me. He gives me one hot, wet, demanding kiss. Then his jaw muscles contract, hot desire flashes in his eyes and he takes possession of my body, inch by inch. I groan from the sensation of the slow stretching and filling of my opening.

My walls somehow accommodate his size and clench around him. As he starts to move inside me, bursts of hot sensation ricochet through my core. This is so intense. I never even imagined sex like this. It's mind-blowing, addicting.

Every thrust delivers another pleasurable thrill deep inside me. The hedonistic sensation intensifies, spreading wider. He grips the back of the seat tighter. His biceps bunch and flex and his dimples deepen. Even his jaw muscles contract as his hips pump harder and faster to transport us to a climactic finish.

I gaze toward where our hips meet and watch his penis sink into my body and retract again. I hear the wet sound of each thrust. It's enough to pitch me over the edge of the precipice. I pant and thrash and bite my lip to keep from screaming with ecstasy the way I want to. As my convulsions of pleasure begin to subside, Luca thrusts one more time, halting his movement during his burst of release.

He stares at me, a satisfied smile on his face. His face is just an inch away, his hot breath on my neck. "Are you enjoying the flight?" he whispers to me, imitating flight attendant speak.

I laugh and kiss him playfully. "Do you really need to ask?"

"Probably not, but I wanted to ask anyway."

"It's amazing. You're amazing." I want to say something else. Like I'm completely crazy about him. Maybe even in love. But it feels too soon. Something could still go wrong. A week ago, I freaked out when things between us heated up. Today, everything is different. Instead of letting fear dampen my enjoyment of life, I allowed myself to just give in to the moment. I wish I could do this more often.

Luca slowly slips out of me. He adjusts my panties and my dress. His touch is gentle and loving. He takes off the condom and discards it in a bag, cleans himself up with a tissue and dresses. He sits down beside me, leans over and gives me a tender kiss on the forehead. "Maybe we should get some sleep, beautiful."

"That's a good idea. Thank you, Luca." My eyelids already feel blissfully heavy. We puff up our pillows, snuggle in close to each other until I can feel his warm breath on my cheek and his strong hand on my back. I feel safe and cared for close to Luca. My lips turn up in a contented smile and before I know it, I'm asleep.

CHAPTER TWENTY-TWO

Jade

After landing in Salzburg, a customs agent boarded the plane to check our passports. Then we were whisked off to a hotel in a luxurious limousine. The ride seemed short. The views on the way to the hotel thrilled me. We drove across a broad river. From the bridge I saw cliffs of rocks, numerous ancient stone buildings and churches with tall towers or tile roofs, and the huge castle on a hill that Luca said he was going to show me tomorrow.

From the balcony in our room, I look out over narrow streets and a nearby church. The bells in the church tower chime, announcing that it's nine in the morning. The long trip is starting to catch up with me. My body feels heavy and tired, my thoughts hazy.

I sag into one of the blue-painted wrought iron chairs and just enjoy the view. Luca steps out of the French doors and smiles when he sees me. His hair hasn't seen a brush, but looks sexy as hell tangled and covering one eye. It's Exhibit A of all the wild things we did on that plane. My hair is Exhibit B. I tried using a brush, but it didn't help much.

"Are you doing okay?"

I raise my hand to mask a yawn. My body says that it's the middle of the night—which it still is in San Carlos. "All those time zone changes are definitely getting to me."

"It will take a few days to get completely used to the time change. But it's better to stay awake as long as we can today so we can start adjusting. And this fresh air should do us good."

"My body clock is definitely off. But I'm too excited to sleep anyway. I'd much rather explore this place with you."

Luca kisses me on top of the head. "Can I tempt you into the shower first?"

I look up at him and smile. That's the only hope for resuscitating my appearance. "Most definitely."

He reaches for my hand. A tug from him gets me on my feet. We walk silently inside. Both of us are barefoot. Like me, he kicked off his shoes almost the minute we got into the room. Already, I'm learning about his habits, some of which are very similar to mine. "It's time for that dress to come off."

He reaches for the hem of my dress and raises it slowly over my thighs, exposing my abdomen, my chest. I raise my arms and allow him to pull it over my head. With a flick of his hand, he tosses it onto the bed. The dress I was wearing had a built-in shelf bra so now I'm standing in front of him, my bare breasts exposed, wearing only pale blue silk panties.

He kneels down in front of me. His fingers skim down my thighs and calves taking my underwear with them, leaving a trail of tingling hot spots behind. I lift one foot and then the other to step out of them. A cool breeze from the open French doors tickles my bare skin. Goose pimples rise on my already excited flesh. "Now it's my turn to undress you," I say.

"Soon. But not yet." His hands skim over the contours of my calves and thighs. "Your skin is so soft. And beautiful. And your legs are shaped so perfectly."

The way he's talking, the way he touches me. He treats me like I'm precious to him, like he adores me. My heart swells with emotion. This man, who I've only known for a few weeks means so much to me already. We seem right for each other in many ways. I never imagined I'd ever have this kind of physical and mental connection with a man. But Luca is here in front of me. Caressing my skin, each stroke of his fingers sending bolts of desire through my body.

He slowly rises to his feet, his hands moving over the swell of my hips, across my tummy toward my exposed breasts.

I slowly unbutton his shirt, delighted to see the firm ridges of his chest appear. He unbuttons the cuffs and I slowly glide the shirt over his broad shoulders, exposing the swell of muscles and his collarbone. His skin is soft to the touch, but his body is solid. I slowly slip the shirt down his back and toss it on the bed beside my dress. I slide my tongue over my lower lip, already salivating over what I'll be exposing next. I undo the button on the tight jeans he's wearing and unzip them slowly. I tug them down over his hips and wrestle them to the floor. He steps out of them and kicks them to the side. The swell of his erection stretches his cotton briefs. He's hard and ready for me and my body reacts right away. Warm arousal dampens my inner thighs. I skim my hands over the length of Luca's still-covered cock. It's so rigid and large, I struggle to remove his underwear.

He gazes down at me. Lust burns in his eyes as he watches me remove his briefs. He takes my hands in his. I slowly rise to my feet. Now there's just the two of us with no clothes between us.

I don't move. I gaze, wide-eyed, at the perfection that is Luca. Everything about him mesmerizes me. His solid, well-hewn body. His blue-green eyes. And that expression on his face. Yellow flecks of desire flash in his eyes. But the gentle tilt of his brows shows he wants more from me than just my body. He reaches for my hand. "Come with me, Jade. Let's take a shower."

I follow him into the bathroom, where there's a large walk-in shower. He turns on the water, and dials it to a very warm temperature just the way I like it. I step under the waterfall of water with him, feeling the warmth flow over my head, neck, shoulders. The warm water feels so soothing after the long flight, slowly loosening all of my tired muscles until they feel relaxed.

He squeezes some shampoo into his hand. I step back from the water. "Close your eyes," he says before he lathers up my hair. His fingertips gently massage the top and the sides and the back of my head, making my mind drift away. It feels good to close my eyes and turn myself over to his touch.

Luca makes me feel so loved. He gently shifts my head back under the water for a rinse. His fingers thread through my hair, skimming across my scalp to release the shampoo from my hair. No man has ever washed my hair before. Hair washing was never one of my romantic fantasies. But this is one of the most romantic experiences I've ever had in my life. Luca's touch makes me feel nurtured and appreciated.

He finishes my hair and leads me away from the shower head again. He lathers up soap on a washcloth. Gently, he washes my face, my ears, my neck. Then the washcloth massages my shoulders and arms.

He raises each of my arms to wash under them. Then he turns me around and lovingly washes my back, my buttocks, my legs. After shifting me into the water to rinse my back, he turns me toward him, smiling when our gazes connect.

He looks so amazing wet. His angular jaw, the dent of his dimples and his firm body look even more defined when they are slick with water. He moves the washcloth over my breasts, my belly. He kneels down in front of me, raising one foot and resting it on his shoulder while he washes it. He touches and washes each toe with such loving care. Then he washes my calf and my thigh. He washes my other leg, but when he finishes, he moves the washcloth between my legs, slowly massaging and spreading me open.

Liquid heat surges through my core, making my legs unsteady. He rinses the soap from the washcloth and moves the washcloth between my legs again. Then he drops the washcloth. It falls to the shower floor with a splash. He buries his face between my legs and flicks his tongue across my slit. I feel a gush of excitement rush southward. He lowers my foot to the floor. "Sit on the ledge," he says in a commanding voice.

Remembering how good it felt to have his mouth on me earlier, I nearly leap toward the ledge. My legs tremble as I seat myself, legs spread, on the marble. Still kneeling, he opens my thighs wide apart and licks my slit again. I gasp with pleasure. This feels so good. He flicks his tongue over my clit, at first slowly and then in a maddening rhythm that makes me squirm with pleasure and want. He slides a finger inside of me. My head falls back in a moan. As he fucks me with his finger, his tongue flicks over my clit again and again. Pleasure ricochets through me, blurring my vision. I'm so turned on my inner walls feel about to explode. In an instant, I fall over the edge. I thrash and moan as waves of ecstasy roll through me. He slowly urges me up from where I'm sitting and turns me around.

"Bend over and grip the sides of the wall for me," he says.

My pussy tightens again. Oh, God, he's going to fuck me from the back. How hot. As I lean over and grab the sides of the ledge, I feel the brush of his cock against my butt. My core clenches with aching need. I arch my back, exposing my pussy to him to give him easy entrance. I want him to take me. I want him to sink deep into me now.

He grips my hips. Too slowly. What are we waiting for? Did he forget to bring a condom in?

"Please, Luca, now."

"Don't worry, Jade. I'll give you what you want."

I hear him rip open a condom package. He spreads me apart with a finger and positions himself at my opening. I feel the tip of his cock pushing into me. I arch my back to increase the penetration. He must know I can't wait a second longer.

He slides deep inside me in one swift drive. He slowly slips out of me, then slams into me again. Pleasure explodes deep inside of me each time he thrusts. I groan and hold onto the sides of the ledge tighter, feeling my hands lose their purchase. He pumps in and out of me, faster and faster. I can hear the slap of water between our hips.

Every nerve ending inside of me screams with pleasure as the head of his cock slams deep inside and his balls rub against my clit. "More, Luca. Oh, yes, don't stop." As Luca's cock slams into me again, I pant and moan as an orgasm blasts through me like dynamite.

He continues moving inside of me until his own release comes. Then his arms slide up to above my waist. He slowly raises me up and turns me to face him. He's still breathing hard.

He looks incredibly hot, his sculpted face and all his rippled muscles slippery wet. His eyes are more blue now than green. And he has a wicked grin on his face. "You are wonderful, Jade." His voice sounds husky.

Even his voice is hot. Then he kisses me on the lips.

This kiss is gentle and filled with emotion, the way his touch was when he washed my hair and body. He knows what I need. He satisfies my desire and also my need for loving touch. He offers that blend of raw sexuality and gentleness that feels right. Almost too right. But I have a way of being blind to the truth. Maybe I just think this is perfect. And what I'm seeing and feeling isn't reality.

CHAPTER TWENTY-THREE

Jade

Our hotel is on a narrow cobblestoned street. We stroll along it, holding hands and admiring what we see in the shop windows. We pass a chocolate shop and an outdoor vendor selling fresh fruit. My eyes widen and my steps slow when we reach a bakery displaying mouth-watering pastries and loaves of freshly baked bread brushed with butter. "Mmm. That bread smells good." I still feel euphoric from our love-making earlier. Now I'm excited to explore the city, my jetlag having flown.

"It does smell good. Are you hungry?" Luca's hair is still wet from our shower. The morning breeze tosses his damp curls against his cheek bones. His eyes are shielded by his aviator glasses.

"Starving."

"Why don't we have lunch before we walk up to the castle," Luca suggests.

"Okay by me."

"Is there anything in particular you're in the mood for?"

"No, not really. I would like to try some local cuisine."

"I know of a few places tucked away off the street on the other side of the river. One of them serves excellent Austrian dishes."

"I would like that."

We walk hand and hand across the bridge. Luca points up at the castle. "That's where we'll be going later."

"It's like something out of a fairy tale."

"It is, but it will be a bit of workout getting up there. There are many steps and some steep trails. Unless you want to take the funicular."

The castle doesn't look that far away. But he's not kidding; it's definitely up a steep incline. "What's a funicular?"

"It's a train that goes straight up. The main disadvantage is that there are long lines and it's very crowded. And…" He pauses for a moment and runs a finger along one of his dimples.

I read his mind. "You're worried you'll be recognized."

"Yes, that's it. I don't like having that happen, especially in crowded spaces where there's no escape. When everyone grabs their phones and starts taking photos of me I have to smile and pretend it doesn't bother me."

I can't even imagine what it would be like to deal with that intrusiveness on a regular basis. I've always been an introvert and sometimes I'm not in the mood to talk to anyone, let alone complete strangers. "Let's not deal with that. A walk will be fine. It's a lovely day."

A cool breeze caresses my shoulders. The scent in the air is a mingling of freshly baked bread, weathered stone, and cigarette smoke.

We walk along another cobblestone street, passing the apartment building where Mozart was born. I wonder what this building looked like 300 years ago. The exterior now shines bright yellow and the trim around the building's many windows glows a clean white. This centuries-old building has been preserved like many others in this city.

Salzburg is filled with history. I've never seen anything like this. It even smells like a different era. A little musty. I like that the city's history is preserved. In the States, anything old is considered obsolete. Buildings, even people. Here age is worthy of respect.

I occasionally bump shoulders with other people crowding the street. And everywhere, there are bicycles. I dodge out of the way of a rider weaving through the walkers. "Watch where you're going," Luca says, angrily, craning his head toward the bicyclist.

"I think it's wonderful that people here use bicycles as a mode of transportation," I say. "But some of them are a little crazy."

"That's for sure." He slings his arm around my shoulder, moving me closer to his body. "Stay near me. I'll keep you safe."

I nuzzle up against his neck, feeling his hair tickle my cheek. "I know you will."

"We're going to get away from all this in a minute anyway."

A narrow side street leads us to the end of the walled walkway, which is surrounded by apartment buildings and restaurants. Vines creep up the sides of the stone walls. All the restaurants have large patios and outdoor tables.

"Here's the place I was thinking of," says Luca. "Does it look okay to you?"

It's quiet and protected from the sun. "It looks great."

A waiter approaches and invites us to choose any table on the outdoor patio. We find a seat and sit across from each other. I admire our surroundings. A group of four people at a table nearby are speaking in another language—German, I presume. Each one of them has a large amber-colored glass in front of them.

Luca takes off his sunglasses and sets them down on the table. He smiles and laugh lines appear at the corners of his eyes. "People start drinking early in Europe, as you can see."

I laugh and lean in closer. "I see that. I read online that alcohol is bad for jetlag, so I think I'll pass."

"That's a very wise choice. It's taken time for me to get the hang of overseas travelling. I adjust much faster to time changes when I change my sleep schedule right away. I also try to drink lots of water and get plenty of fresh air and exercise."

"That makes sense. I will do my best to follow all your expert advice."

We talk more about adjusting to the time change and when the waiter comes by, we both order sparkling water. Luca persuades me to order the Wiener Schnitzel—a veal cutlet that has been breaded and fried. "It's not the healthiest meal in the world," he says, "but it's my favorite Austrian dish."

My mouth waters when the waiter sets my plate down in front of me. There's a huge piece of veal on my plate just waiting for me to slice into it. Arranged on the plate beside it is a chunky potato salad and some salad greens. The meal looks delicious and smells even better. "Wow. This looks really tasty."

Luca is already slicing into his meat. He smiles at me as he chews a bite. He watches me, eager to see me take a taste.

I slice off a piece of the veal. The tender meat dissolves in my mouth with a burst of juicy flavor. I chew slowly to savor the taste. "Delicious. I'm glad you suggested this. When were you last here?"

"Last October. This is my sixth time in Salzburg. I usually come here or go to Sorrento before our tours start. The guys and I have worked out this plan where we come at least two days early so we're used to the time change and at our best for our first performance."

"I can see why you like to come here. It's beautiful. I love all of the old buildings. I'll have to go online later and read more about Salzburg's history."

"This is an old city, steeped in history. Much of Europe is like this. You walk through the street, seeing so many old churches and castles and feel like you've stepped back in time. And whenever I'm in Europe, especially Italy, I remember my childhood. The good times, mostly." He gazes off in the distance, looking reflective.

"Tell me what you remember, Luca. I'd like to hear more."

"My two brothers and I spent our summers outside. There were a group of guys we'd meet at a park near our house. We'd play soccer every night until it was too dark to see the ball anymore. One evening when we were walking home, a musician was performing in front of one of the fountains.

Intrigued, I stopped to listen. I was only eight at the time. My impatient brothers wouldn't wait for me. I started humming along to the tune he was playing on his guitar. I still remember the man had silver hair twisted into dreadlocks. He waved for me to come over and told me his name was Alessandro. After that I met him in the park every day. He said I had an ear for music. He taught me how to read music and how to play guitar. Sometimes I'd make up lyrics to go with his tunes."

"That's amazing how meeting this man helped you find your gift."

"I was lucky I found him. Alessandro was a wonderful man."

"When did you start taking music lessons?"

"I never had any formal training in music until we moved to Mexico. After my father left us."

"Do you know where your father is now?"

"No. And I don't want to know." He clenches his jaw and fidgets with his water glass.

I reach for his hand under the table. "I'm sorry. I shouldn't have asked that."

"Don't worry. It was a long time ago." Despite his reassurance, the hint of sadness remains in his eyes. "I sometimes worry I might see him somewhere when I'm Sorrento. I'm not sure what I would say if I ran into him at a grocery store or a café. Would I pretend I didn't recognize him and just walk away? Or would I confront him and ask him why he deserted us? He probably wouldn't even recognize me. I haven't seen him since I was a boy. It's not knowing why he left that still haunts me. It seems inconceivable that any man would walk away from my mother. She is so beautiful. And she is kind and honest and loving."

"I'm sorry, Luca. There probably was no good reason. He probably couldn't handle the responsibility."

"I think you're right." He sighs. Then he pauses for a moment while the waiter comes by and scoops up our empty plates. He gives me a boyish grin. "Do you have room for dessert? You might like the Apfelstrudel, but my favorite is the Sacher Torte."

"I know about apple strudel, but what's the other one?"

"The most delicious chocolate cake."

I burst out laughing. "Luca, are you serious? I figured with your body, you never eat an ounce of fat or sugar."

"I do enough running and weight training that I can afford to enjoy a good meal once in a while. We had quite a workout earlier. And we have a long walk ahead of us. So, what do you say? You want to sample something sweet and Austrian?" One of his thick brows raises mischievously.

"Hell, yes, I do."

He laughs. "You're my kind of girl."

Minutes later, we're both eating cake. I can't help smiling when I see the way Luca's eyes flash brilliant green when he takes a bite. A large dark crumb sits on the edge of his lips. I want to lick it off. And kiss him until I can taste the chocolate on his mouth and tongue.

CHAPTER TWENTY-FOUR

Jade

After lunch, we walk toward Festung Hohensalzburg. We climb several flights of stone stairs and then follow the steep, winding path on up. As we ascend higher and higher, the crowds start to thin. Soon all we can hear is the whisper of wind in the meadows and the occasional chime of a church bell.

Alongside the path are a few small stone houses. Tall trees provide shade, and in the stretches of meadow, tall grass and flowers bow in the breeze. A sign directs us toward the castle. "Before we visit the castle, I want to show you this view," says Luca.

We walk hand in hand to the top of the hill and stand beside each other admiring the panorama. "This is beautiful." I glance at Luca and squeeze his hand. Beyond acres and acres of green fields, a jagged front of snow-capped mountains pierces the sky. "Come over here. Let's sit on this wall for a moment."

Luca sits beside me on the stone wall, close enough that our shoulders touch. He doesn't say a word. I don't mind that he's quiet. I feel so emotionally connected to him right now. No words seem necessary. I still feel that special bond I always feel when we're together. I know he notices the whisper of the wind in the grass and the chirping birds.

He, like me, appreciates peace, appreciates nature. That's what drew him to San Carlos. The places he chooses to rest before his Europe tours are similarly serene. That's what he needs to keep his life in balance.

He jumps down from the wall and reaches for my hand. "Come on. Let's go check out the castle."

We walk together down the road until we see the massive wooden doors, dotted with rusted metal bolts, that mark the castle's entrance. Enormous stone walls surround most of the castle. There are turrets and flat stone walls. Windows poke through many of the walls that must be at least three feet thick. The stone is blackened by hundreds of years of exposure to the elements.

Once we pay the entrance fee, we're handed headsets and a remote that we can use to take the walking tour. We stroll from room to room, hearing about the history of this place—one of the largest medieval castles in Europe. The floorboards squeak beneath my feet. An odor of damp stone lingers in the air. The place is ancient. The stone is washed in a faint black ash.

We peer into many musty-smelling rooms with stone walls and wooden floors. One of the rooms, once used for a torture chamber, contains a wagon wheel, which was dropped on the bodies of the hapless victims to break their bones. A shiver rolls through me as I look around the room.

The overlooks are my favorite. We climb narrow, winding flights of stairs to reach them. From the top of the castle we look out at the high cliffs that rim the hills, the meandering Salzach River and the sea of spires and domes around the city. I'm awed by the amazing architecture in Salzburg—the blocky buildings with their dozens of windows and the blue onion domes and red tile rooftops that cap them.

The recording tells us that the construction of the castle began in 1077 and during the time of the Holy Roman Empire, the archbishops of Salzburg made more improvements. Eventually, the fort was captured by French troops. In the nineteenth century, it was used as barracks, storage depot and dungeon before being abandoned as a military outpost in 1861.

The audio tour ends when we're on top of one of the buildings. We both take our headsets off and stand beside each other, admiring the view.

The wind lifts my hair and brushes against my face. It's warm, but not hot. A perfect day. This spot gives us a 360-degree view of the city. It seems too amazing to be real—this beautiful city of ancient buildings backed by the snowy Alps. The adventurer in me wants to get closer to those mountains, to hike up their flanks and pick a flower. “Have you ever seen the Alps up close?”

“Yes, a few times. I’ve hiked and rented an e-bike before.”

“What’s an e-bike?”

“It’s an electric bike. They’re used often by tourists in the Alps. You still pedal, but the motor helps you along more or less, depending on what level you choose. E-bikes make steep hills much more bearable and are great for exploring.”

“It sounds like a blast.”

“We could go to the mountains tomorrow if you like and give it a try.”

“Seriously? I would love that.”

“I’ll reserve some bikes later on.”

I turn and kiss him on the lips. “Oh, Luca, you have no idea how much fun I’m having on this trip already.”

He grips my shoulders and looks at me with a soft, loving gaze. "I'm glad you're having a good time. It's wonderful having you with me on this tour."

I wonder what it would be like to stand up on a stage in front of thousands of people. I can't imagine it, really. I'd probably be so terrified, I'd forget the words to every song. "Do you ever get nervous when you perform?"

"Most of the time, I feel stressed an hour or two before the performance. Once I'm up on stage, I get so lost in the music, I forget my worries. This is what I do, I perform. It all comes naturally now."

"Tell me what happened after you moved to Mexico. That's when you started taking voice lessons, right?"

"My mom found out I'd been learning some things from Alessandro shortly before everything went to hell. She tried to persuade me to take voice lessons, but I kept saying I didn't want to."

"Why, Luca?"

"I wanted to more than anything. But I was the oldest. I understood the financial hardships my mother was dealing with. My mamá made many sacrifices for me, but I couldn't let her go that far. My brothers and sisters had needs too."

Most young people would only be concerned about their own needs. But not Luca. His mother taught him well to look out for his family. "Was your mother upset?"

"Yes, very. She told me I had talent and that she didn't want me wasting it. We went back and forth over it for several months. Then I had a stroke of luck. I had just started middle school and I told my mamá I would join the choir and try out for any afterschool programs that were offered.

I always auditioned for solo parts. And did quite well performing them at concerts. One day, my teacher, Mr. González, asked me to stay after class. He said I was gifted and that I should consider formal musical training. I told him about our family's financial situation. He persuaded me to let him pay for me to take voice lessons twice weekly in exchange for me help teaching his son to play the guitar. I agreed and kept this arrangement a secret from my mother for several months. Even though I was giving something back, I worried it would hurt her pride to find out I was accepting financial help.

"Eventually, I felt too guilty, keeping all this a secret from her. My mamá burst into tears when I confessed to her. But after I explained how I had taught Mr. González's son, Miguel, how to play the guitar, she didn't seem as upset. She went to my school to talk to him. When he told her how talented I was and what a help I had been to his son, she came home with tears in her eyes. She said she was very proud of me."

"Did you keep on taking lessons after that?"

"I did. My teacher connected me with other musicians. My brother was already playing in the band. I auditioned a few people, chose a group of guys, and formed my own band. Steve joined us later, but Raphael, Lorenzo and Larry have been playing with me since I was seventeen."

"You all seem to get along well."

"Lorenzo's my brother, of course. But the rest of them—they're like an extension of my family. We've spent a lot of time on the road together and it just keeps on getting better. This gig has worked out great for all of us. We all came from poor families. Steve was homeless when I found him performing on the street in Los Angeles. By then, I had an agent and we'd already had two albums hit platinum in the US.

We all worked hard to turn our lives around. And we've all been able to help our struggling families live an easier life."

I'm awed by his rags-to-riches story and touched at how much it obviously mattered to him to be able to help his family. Luca is the most amazing man I've ever met. The more I find out about him, the more I love him.

He frowns, lost in thought. I am puzzled. Everything he's saying is how his whole life went from difficult to a dream because of his amazing talent. "What is it?"

He reaches for me and his fingers softly caress my face. "Everything changed suddenly. I went from worrying about where our next meal would come from to having more money than I could ever spend. Sometimes it doesn't seem real. I worry it might all suddenly come to an end. I have recurring nightmares about walking up on stage to loud boos. What if I bumble an interview or a false tabloid post comes out? Will my fans abandon me? I'm not really the person they see on stage."

This confession surprises me. Luca always seems so confident. I never imagined that he, like me, struggles with doubt. Maybe it's the rejection we suffered when we were children. It's hard to trust in anything when you've seen how quickly things can go wrong.

Luca has such remarkable talent. He has fans on every continent. I can't imagine anything with his career could ever go wrong. "I understand why you have doubts, especially after everything you've been through as a child. But I think you're selling yourself short. I like you just the way you are very much. And you express many of your deepest feelings in your music and your fans can't get enough of you."

"Thank you, Jade. I appreciate your kind words."

"I mean it, Luca. I know more than anyone how hard it is to believe in yourself. But you're such a star. You have no idea how excited I am to see you on stage. I can't wait."

Luca leans in and kisses me on the cheek. "It will be great to see your face out there."

A shiver of excitement rolls through me as I imagine watching Luca up there on that stage wowing the crowds.

He'll be thinking of me while he's up there. Won't he? And he'll notice me out there in the crowd.

Suddenly, a cloud passes over the sun. The breeze raises goosebumps on my arms and shoulders and I shiver.

CHAPTER TWENTY-FIVE

Jade

I'm sitting in a front-row seat at the Vienna Boys' Choir concert hall. Luca's up on stage, wearing a white collared shirt and tight black pants. He tossed his black jacket onto the stage toward the end of the last song, which brought shrieks of excitement from the female members of the audience.

He performed this sexy striptease act in an amusing way, with a poking-fun-at-himself smile and overexaggerated sways of his hips that incited laughter. Once he shucked off the jacket, he unbuttoned the top three buttons on his shirt, removed his cufflinks and dropped them into his pocket and pushed up his shirtsleeves, revealing his muscular forearms.

When a woman tossed a pair of thong underwear up on stage, the sudden sting of jealousy I experienced quickly subsided after Luca picked them up and pulled them on over his pants, did a 360 degree turn like he was modeling. How he did that without missing a beat in the song, I'll never know.

When everyone laughed, he shook his head, slipped them off and tossed them aside. Then he held the microphone up to his mouth, joked about fashion issues when sweating profusely up on stage, and introduced the next song.

His eyes closed, his forehead creased, he sings with so much energy and passion. Even now that he's lightened up his clothing load, his face is drenched with sweat. The purplish stage lights exaggerate the sexy dimples around his mouth.

I tap my foot on the wooden floors to the beat of the music. I feel the rhythm of this song move through me. I've loved every number Luca's performed.

No wonder he's achieved worldwide fame. He's beyond talented. Listening to his songs online was incredible. But hearing him perform in person is something I'll never forget. I can see and feel his emotions. Every expression on his face, every lyric that he sings, every movement of his body delivers a deep and profound experience.

I dab my eyes with a tissue when he sings a song dedicated to his mother. He sings of how she cared for him, how her love for him made it possible for him to become the man he is today.

I wonder if other people in the audience notice more than the melodic swell of each note and the unique rhythm of his music. Do they understand each word he's saying, are they—like me—experiencing the depth of his feelings?

I glance around me to gauge people's reactions to Luca's performance. People are swaying to the music, clapping their hands, even singing along.

My eyes land on a gray-haired man in the audience who doesn't seem moved by the performance. He's at least 20 years older than the rest of the crowd. His arms are crossed over his chest, he has a scowl on his face. What could he be upset about? Everyone's having such a good time. I look away for a moment and then study the man's face again. There's something about him that looks vaguely familiar. But I can't put a finger on where I've seen him before.

CHAPTER TWENTY-SIX

Jade

Between songs, Luca entertains the audience with short anecdotes and humor. He speaks in English, then in German. He does a stellar job of connecting with the concert goers. He announces the final song of the night. "This song is for a beautiful lady who matters very much to me. This is Jade's Song," he says. And then his gaze locks on me and he blows a kiss in my direction.

My mouth falls open and I clutch my chest. For a moment I forget to breathe. It moved me so much when he told me he wrote a song about me swimming with dolphins. But now he's going to perform this song—with me here—in front of everyone. Many things that he's said and done have rocked my world. He's touched me in ways I never imagined a person could. But this moment. He's announced in front of everyone that this song is just for me.

The instrumental introduction ends. The rich tonality of his voice meets my ears. And the lyrics. They're about me swimming in the sea with the dolphins. Hearing the depth of feeling in his deep voice, watching the sway of his body matching the beat of the music, I feel his heart reaching for mine in every note that he sings. I allow his tenor voice to move through me.

Mysterious woman, she swims in the sea

So strong, so free

Surrounded by dolphins

Surrounded by blue-green sea

She looks free

The way I want to be.

He wrote this song from the depth of his heart. I hear it. Feel it. He loves me. The real me. The woman who loves the sea, who swims with dolphins, who came to Mexico on a whim.

That's why he's sharing this song he wrote for me with the whole world. To express his feelings loud and clear. His voice speaks to my heart. I never imagined being with a man could make me feel like this.

Why did I ever doubt him? He's made it clear how much he cares for me. Luca is different from other men. I don't have to worry any more. I can just enjoy every minute we share. We'll have many days and years together even though his career means we'll sometimes be apart. There will always be the excitement of coming together again, a renewal of that flame that burns so strongly between us that it can't possibly ever burn out. I thought I needed to hide from men. But what I needed was to wait until I found the right one. And how he's up on the stage. Singing about how much I move him.

When the song ends, everyone in the crowd jumps to their feet. There's a roar of applause. They absolutely love him. He thanks the audience and waits for the noise to diminish before announcing they'll do an encore. He's wearing an ear-to-ear smile when he blows me another kiss. I blow one back to him. His gaze scans the audience, then stops.

But now he's not looking at me. The lines around his jaw tighten. His posture looks suddenly rigid. Something has upset him. I look around me, trying to figure out what has distracted him. And then my eyes land on the man I saw before. Oh, my God. Now I know where I've seen him before. I've seen him every time I've looked at Luca. He has the same muscular build. The same chiseled facial features. That man in the audience must be Luca's father.

CHAPTER TWENTY-SEVEN

Luca

When I see my father's face out there in the audience, hot anger surges up from deep inside me. *Cómo pudo hacer esta*? How could he do this? My heart thunders in my chest so hard I hear it in my ears. All the sounds out in the crowd seem muted. He can't be here. *Ahora no*. Not now.

Just minutes ago, I shared my new song with my European audience. Jade's song. It was such a rush, singing those lyrics while my heart was so full of love for her. I wanted to share my deep feelings for her with my audience and to have them know that she is here. Jade is the one I want to spend my life with. Yet all the beauty of tonight's experience was instantly snuffed when I saw my father's face.

His presence ruins everything. I don't want to relive the pain of his desertion. I don't want to face him. He must want to talk to me. Is he going to ask for my forgiveness? Will he ask for money?

A drumroll from Steve snaps me out of my thoughts. The audience has quieted down. I haven't said a single word. I clear my throat. Introduce the encore song. My voice sounds strange and robotic. A strange silence falls over the crowd. I should pull it together, and not allow my father's presence to throw me off like this. Already, I feel myself losing my connection with the audience. All that excitement we built performing Jade's song is gone.

The finale falls flat on the audience. The words flow from my lips, but there's no heart behind them. I'm so overwrought, all I'm thinking about is getting through the song. Part way through the number, Lorenzo steps up to the microphone to accompany me. Hearing his voice supporting mine boosts my morale. Does he know our father is out there in the audience? Maybe together we can face this.

I walk off stage with a splitting headache and a sense of panic. Backstage, reporters have gathered. Where is our press agent? He's supposed to keep them away until our limo arrives, so I only have to say a few short comments.

I look around for Lorenzo. I don't see him anywhere. Steve, Raphael and Larry are still onstage, packing up their equipment. I should have waited for them. Now, I'll have to face the reporters alone.

I stride briskly toward the dressing room. My vocal chords ache. My throat feels like the Sahara Desert. It's time for my usual salt water rinse and tall glass of ice-cold coconut water. Jade's influence.

A reporter races up to me and sticks a microphone in my face. "Your performance had so much energy," says the bald man with large round glasses. "The crowd was going crazy out there."

"Thank you," I say.

"But then you lost it. All that momentum you built up was just gone. What happened?"

I don't want to talk about this performance that could have been one of my best and then, thanks to my father, turned out to be *horrible*. I clench my jaw, willing myself not to break. "I have no comment."

"Are you sick?"

I grasp at the straw he's offered. "It's just a stomach bug, nothing to worry about. But I need to get to my dressing room." I hate telling a falsehood, but if I can get this reporter off my back, the white lie will be worth it. I step around the man, but another woman hops in front of me, taking his place.

"Did you see someone out in the audience from your past? Like an ex-girlfriend, perhaps?" the female reporter asks.

I hear the backstage door open and close. I whip my head in that direction, hoping to see my press agent or my brother or someone who can help me. It's Jade. The instant I see her, some of my anxiety fades. She makes a beeline toward me, an angry look on her face.

"Please," she says in a firm, authoritative voice. She pushes past the reporters and grips my arm. "He needs to go backstage to have a minute to breathe and get rehydrated. Can't you see he's exhausted?"

"Can you comment on what happened out there?" the male reporter asks.

Jade tucks a lock of loose hair behind her ear. "It was an amazing performance. But hearing him perform that song for me with so much feeling." She pauses and presses her lips together. Emotion thickens her voice. "It was one of the best moments of my life. And it was obvious the audience loved it, too."

"But after that, he fell apart," the woman declares.

Jade holds her head high. She doesn't blink once when she speaks. "I don't know what you're talking about." She tugs on my arm to move me away from them. "I have no further comments."

"You're both hiding something. What is it?" asks the man.

The door opens again and my father steps toward us.

CHAPTER TWENTY-EIGHT

Luca

My mouth tastes like metal. The room sways. Jade grips my arm tighter to steady me. *No es posible*. My father can't be here. This can't be happening. I never wanted to see him again. These reporters will figure out that he's my weakness, the one person who can destroy me. My father's lips twist into a self-satisfied smile as he approaches the reporters.

"It seems I'm just in time for the interviews."

The three reporters turn toward him. I look at Jade. Her eyes widen with panic. She knows I'm in trouble, and I don't think she's sure how to handle this either.

"Who is this?" a female reporter asks.

I can't speak. My mouth—and every muscle in my body are frozen.

The man who shares many of my facial features stares at me when he answers the question. "I'm Luca's father."

Jade releases my arm and steps toward the reporters. "We need all of you to leave. Luca hasn't seen his father for a long time and, uh, this is a private moment."

The bald man leans toward Jade. "How long has it been since he's seen his father?"

"Like I said, this is a private matter. Now if you'll excu—"

"I can let you in on a dirty little secret. He stopped speaking to me when he got rich and famous. Thinks he's too good for his old man now."

"Why are you lying?" Jade bursts out. "You abandoned Luca's mother as well as Luca and his brothers and sister when they were just kids."

My stomach twists into knots. I taste bile. I'm not sure what to do. I want him gone. I'm afraid if I say something or get too close to him, I'll rip him apart. I have so much suppressed rage buried deep inside.

"Is that what he told you? His mother was nothing but a slut. I left her because she was sleeping with other men and I'd had enough. For some reason, Luca's always wanted to protect her. Even though she's a worthless bitch. He's a very good liar." My father smirks when he looks at Jade. His gaze sweeps the length of her body.

He shouldn't look at her like he's imagining all her soft curves naked. She belongs to me. I need to protect her from men like my father. I bunch my hands into fists and grit my teeth. I want to break every bone in his body right now, and I'll do it too, if he doesn't shut up.

"He probably told you that you're the only woman in his life too, I suppose. But he's just like his mother. He never stays with anyone for long."

The color drains from Jade's face. Her mouth falls open. She glances from my father to me. "It's not true," I say. My voice cracks when I speak. "Any of it."

My father's piercing laugh makes the hairs on the back of my neck stand up.

The door opens again. It's my press agent, Jorge. "What's going on here?" he demands.

"You're supposed to keep them out." My voice sounds broken.

"Out. All of you. Now." Jorge doesn't take no for an answer. He grips one reporter by the shoulder and turns him toward the door. Finally, they all leave. But the damage has been done. They will run straight to their newspapers and TV stations. I'll be ruined. I knew this might happen. It's always been a nagging thought in the back of my mind. Even worse is seeing the expression on Jade's face. I can see the conflict in her wide, hurt eyes. She doesn't know what or whom to believe.

I take a step toward her and reach for her arm. She takes a step back.

"Do you want me to throw him out?" Jorge asks. "I heard he was in the audience. He was talking to reporters before the concert. I wanted to keep him from getting to you. I'm sorry I got here too late."

I give my father a cold stare. "That's okay, Jorge. Let's find out what it is the man wants. Probably just money."

Jade looks paler than ever. "I'm going to step outside. Give you some privacy to talk."

"You don't need to. I—"

"It would be better if you left." My father speaks dismissively to Jade like she's a servant.

"Don't talk to her like that," I shout.

My father just laughs.

Jade opens the door and closes it quietly behind her. My heart feels torn apart. I know she's suffering. She's probably trying to decide whether what my father said is true.

Her ex treated her like garbage. She's learned to expect that kind of treatment from men. If only there was some way I could convince her I love her. I don't want to lose her. She means so much to me. She needs me, and I want to be there for her. I want to prove to her that I care.

I turn toward my father. My body trembles with rage. How dare he show up here like this? "How much do I need to pay you to stay out of my life forever? I can write you a check right n—"

"Is that any way to speak to your father?"

"How can you walk in here like this after all you've done? And you have the nerve to lie to my girlfriend and speak to her like she's a servant."

"I didn't mean anything by it. I just wanted to talk to you alone."

I grind my teeth together. He didn't mean anything by it? He didn't read the suffering or the simmering anger on our faces? Is this man who calls himself my father a complete idiot? "We have nothing to discuss."

"Maybe I just want to be part of your life again."

"You must be joking. You said you loved me. Then you left. I was only a kid. But I didn't get to be one for long. I had to help mom. She needed me. I was there when you weren't."

My father shuffles his feet nervously. "I admit I made some mistakes. But you can forgive me, right?"

"No, I can't. I still don't understand why you're here. You say you don't want my money. Then what is it you want?"

"I think we can help each other."

Here it comes. He's finally going to spill what he wants, which has nothing to do with a relationship with me. "How's that?"

"I'm launching a new online business. With you behind it, it will succeed for sure."

He can't be serious? "I don't get it."

"It's simple, really. We let the past go. Move forward. And you talk me up to the media whenever you can."

Anger burns like an out of control bonfire in my gut. I've never hated anyone more in my life. I lean in closer. "I won't do it."

His lips twist into a sneer. "I think you will."

I grab him by the collar and jerk hard. "And I'm telling you I won't."

He tries unsuccessfully to push me away. "If you don't give me what I want, I'll destroy you. Your career, your relationship with that slut, Jade. You already set the stage for a fall tonight after you saw me. Your whole performance fell apart."

A sarcastic laugh escapes my lips. "You obviously didn't think this through very well, did you? Trashing me to reporters before you got what you wanted. But I would never help you—even if you hadn't already made that mistake."

He looks momentarily confused and then I see an up-to-no-good flash in his eyes. "I'm sure we can pay them off."

Like a flame doused with gasoline, I explode. I shove him across the room. When he stumbles to the ground, I lunge toward him. "I'm going to fucking kill you if you don't get out of here this minute." I lift him by the collar and retract my fist.

The sneer hasn't left his face, but the tremor in his jaw shows fear. "Are you sure you want me to leave here bleeding?"

He's got me there. I drop him into a crumpled heap onto the floor. "Do whatever you have to do because I will never say that you are part of my life. Never. I don't even imagine you even recognized Lorenzo on stage."

I swing away and storm toward the door. What if he really does destroy me? What if I lose my career? I'll have let Lorenzo and the other guys in my band down. What if I lose Jade? The woman I want to spend the rest of my life with.

My shoulders sag in despair. But I can't let my father manipulate me. My mother taught me to stand up for what is right. If I had allowed my father to draw me into his schemes, I would have become a different man. There would have been nothing left of me.

CHAPTER TWENTY-NINE

Jade

The three reporters rush me the instant I step outside. I don't want to talk to anyone. I need time to think. I'm confused. An hour ago, when Luca performed Jade's song, a thrill raced through me. I was sure we'd be together forever. Now I'm drowning in doubt. His father's here. And he says Luca's been lying. I don't think that's true, but how do I know for sure? I thought I could trust Brandon—right up to the minute he humiliated me in front of everyone at the restaurant.

But Luca has proved he cares for me. He's been kind and compassionate and real. And I love him. But there's no future for us as awful as it is to imagine being without him. Even though Luca wants me in his life now, he won't once the media expose all my vulnerabilities and pick me to pieces.

I won't be able to flash stunning smiles and toss out witty lines like everyone would expect the woman in a famous man's life to do. I don't feel that confident yet. Maybe I never will. It's not fair for me to prolong our relationship under those circumstances.

Luca might feel obligated to stay with me even if I drag him down. Tonight was disastrous enough for him. I want Luca to get through this media frenzy that will undoubtedly follow.

Having me in news interviews would only make things worse.

I feel so alone right now. I don't want to be here, in Vienna, thousands of miles from home. I want to be back in my seaside condo in San Carlos where I feel safe. I want to take my daily swims and get back to my quiet life where no one notices me. And where no one can ever hurt me again.

"Is that man really Luca's father?" a woman asks.

I hear ringing in my ears. My hands are clammy. I feel desperate to run. "I have no comment," I say as I walk past them.

"How long have you been Luca's girlfriend?" a woman asks.

I don't answer, but the reporters keep following me.

A bald male reporter steps in front of me. "Luca's never written a song for any woman he's been with before. He must be serious about you. He's usually with a different girl on every tour." He says it like he knows this for sure. I suppose Luca's his beat.

The other reporters close in. I feel claustrophobic and panicked. Completely insane, actually. I rub my hands together and hope they won't hear the tremor in my voice. I'm going to lose my mind if I don't get out of here. "Was there a question in there someplace? Look, I have nothing more to say."

The bald man bumps against my shoulder. "What are your plans for the future?"

Drops of sweat bead up on my forehead. My body starts to shake. I can't talk to them anymore. Not for an instant longer. "I said I have nothing else to say. Please, leave me alone." But they don't leave. Now the subtle shaking in my body has turned violent. My jaw aches from clenching my teeth. I've never liked crowds. And

I definitely don't like being surrounded by strange people who keep asking me questions I'm not prepared to answer.

My panic just proves that I'm not the right woman for Luca. If I were, I'd be able to handle myself better. I'd calmly answer all their questions. I wouldn't let their pushiness unravel me. But I'm not calm. Every minute talking to these reporters is ripping me apart. I don't like it. Maybe on a different day, I could handle this better. But not today. I feel short of breath. I need air. I have to escape. Now.

I shove the bald man away. He knocks over two other reporters like he was a bowling ball and they were pins. And then I run. Away from all of them. I run across the stage, jump down into the auditorium and race to the back of the room.

When I exit the building, I barely notice the honk of horns and the screech of brakes as I dash across the street. I don't stop. I don't respond to the angry voices. I keep on running.

CHAPTER THIRTY

Luca

I chug the coconut water and grab my jacket off the chair in the dressing room. I leave the room to find the backstage area empty. My father is gone. *Gracias a Dios* for that. I rush out the door to the stage looking for Jade. My gaze sweeps the room. The wooden floors are bare. The stage crew has removed all of our equipment and already swept the floors. The auditorium seats are empty. It's as if tonight's concert never happened.

"Jade, are you here?" My voice echoes in the high-ceilinged auditorium. There's no answer. I walk to the front of the stage and jump down to the floor. I walk briskly up the aisle and look around the auditorium.

A text message pops up on my phone. I eagerly pull it out of my pocket, hoping it's from Jade. But it's Lorenzo. He wants to know what's holding me up. He and the guys are waiting in the limo. I call him back and ask if he's seen Jade.

He says he hasn't. He says he heard about all the drama with our dad showing up and that they had to drive around the block twice already to shake off pursuing reporters. I tell him they can go ahead and leave for the hotel. I have to find Jade, I tell him. My brother asks if I want help with the search. I tell him no, but I ask him to check to see if she's returned to the hotel.

After I conclude the call, I try Jade's cell phone. It goes straight to voice mail. I contact the hotel and ask to be connected to our room. There's no answer there either. I leave the concert hall and walk out on the street. A misty rain is falling. I look right and left, hoping I'll see Jade standing by a light pole or glancing into a shop window. The streets of Vienna are well lit, the streets clogged with traffic.

People walk past me, oblivious to my distress. At least no one recognizes me. A bus pulls up to a stop in front of me. Several people disembark. I'm surrounded by faces. But I don't see the one face I want to see. I don't see Jade.

Maybe she's given up on me after all. I don't blame her. It's true there were affairs. But they meant nothing to me. They satisfied a physical need but left me emotionally empty. Ever since I met Jade, my heart has belonged to her. I love her so much. I love her too much to lose her now. I'm going to fight for what we have. I'm going to fight to prove I'm the right man for her and that we're meant to be together.

I walk down the street looking for her, fighting off my feelings of panic. Where is she? Worried thoughts nag at my belly. Is she alone in the night somewhere? What if she's lost? Or someone grabbed her purse? She could be in danger. If only I knew where she was. Even if we're no longer a couple, I have to make sure she's safe. The rain falls harder until I can hear it pelting the street and the nearby rooftops. I have no umbrella and my light jacket isn't meant for the rain.

My phone vibrates in my pocket. I grab it and see it's a text from Jade. *Dios mío*. Where she is? Did she somehow know I was worrying about her? I blink through the water dripping from my eyelashes, desperate to see what her message says.

I'm sorry about tonight. I know it was awful for you. I'm sorry I ran away. I wanted to be there for you, but I just couldn't. I'm on my way to the airport. I have to get out of here. I can't face any more reporters. I'd only make things worse for you. I wish I could be stronger – for you and for me – but I'm not meant for this kind of life. You need a stronger woman, someone who can talk to the press without having a nervous breakdown. I enjoyed our time together, Luca, more than you will ever know. I'll be okay. And I hope you will be, too.

The message ends with a heart icon. My heart feels like it's been ripped from my chest. It's over. How could this have happened? If only I'd been able to keep her from leaving that room. Then at least I would have had a chance to talk to her before she left.

I never expected her to have to talk to reporters all the time. I could have arranged for a private bodyguard so she would have been sheltered from most of the media attention. But she never gave me a chance. I've done everything possible to prove to her I care, but I can't make this work if she's not even willing to give us a chance.

Despair threatens to pull me under. I've always felt like I had a measure of control over my life, like I could do something to right whatever was wrong. I felt that way even after my father abandoned us. I was young and strong and passionate. I loved my family so much, and I was determined to help them. Now I feel like I'm being pushed down a swift moving stream. About to tumble over the edge of a waterfall.

CHAPTER THIRTY-ONE

Jade

The taxi driver turns off at the exit to the airport. I just sent Luca a text message. I feel like a knife just sliced open my heart. It hurts even worse to think about how what I've done is affecting him. He's had such a horrible night already, and I'm sure my message is making it much worse. I can only hope in a few months both of our wounds will start to heal. We'll look back and realize that this relationship never could have worked. And we'll always have memories of the days we spent together. They were some of the best days of my life.

I wish I didn't feel so conflicted. I keep wondering if I'm making a mistake. Connections like Luca and I have don't happen every day. We talk to each other, we understand each other, and the sex is mind-blowing.

I wasn't expecting his father to show up and that sudden rush of reporters. Anyone would have found that situation difficult. But I panicked and ran away. I made my choice and now there's no turning back. Luca won't forgive me after what I've done. I'm going to have to live with my decision.

At the airport, I approach an airline counter and ask about a ticket. I wince when she tells me the cost and lists all the long layovers. It's going to take nearly two days to get to Hermosillo. Then I'll still have to hire a taxi to take me the rest of the way to San Carlos. Fine, I tell her. And place my credit card on the counter. I'll pay it off eventually. At least all this will be behind me soon. After walking to the gate, I sit and wait for the boarding announcement. I'm relieved that no one recognizes me as Luca's girlfriend. Or as his ex-girlfriend, I think miserably. I'm sure tomorrow the shit will hit the fan and more than likely the whole world will hear about our bitter ending. I shiver at the unpleasant thought.

After the flight to JFK departs, I take a sleeping pill. Gradually, the tension ebbs from my muscles, the racing thoughts in my brain slow, and the edges of my emotions blur. I feel only a dull haze instead of the overwhelming agony of the empty hole where my heart is supposed to be. It's a relief to just stop thinking, to stop feeling. Soon I drift into a drugged sleep.

I awaken to the sound of voices and the bitter smell of coffee. I open my eyes, see the bright light in the cabin and people moving about. I don't want to be awake. Every muscle in my body hurts. My head throbs. But what pains me the most is remembering. Luca isn't with me now. The empty ache in my chest is more noticeable than ever. I miss him. His laugh. His smile. His masculine scent. The way he always says things that make everything feel right. I swipe away a tear with the back of my hand.

The flight attendant serves me a cup of coffee. My headache slowly subsides. I take a few bites of yogurt and leave the rest of my food untouched.

After we land, I clear customs and rush toward my connecting gate to Dallas. I still have to go there and to Mexico City before Hermosillo. There's no luggage to transfer. I left it all behind in Vienna.

I wonder what Luca's doing right now. Is he upset that I left? Have the reporters written things that will damage his career? I wonder what they said about me. Will they write me off as just one more flavor of the week? I see a kiosk selling newspapers. Should I check to see if there's a story? I slow down and for a moment and then decide against it. Not now.

CHAPTER THIRTY-TWO

Luca

All night long, I toss and turn, thinking of Jade. It feels wrong not having her in bed beside me. I wish I could taste her lips and touch her skin. Instead, next to me is an empty pillow and cold sheets that make me long for the warmth of her beautiful body. I thrash around for hours until I'm entangled in the sheets by morning. I drag my leaden body out of bed and stumble into the kitchenette to brew coffee.

I think again about Jade, wondering and worrying. Did she make it home safely? I'm worried about Mamá, too, and what the press will say about her. My father said so many awful things about her.

Of course, his words were all lies. He was nasty to Jade, too, which makes no sense. He doesn't even know her. After all that he had the nerve to ask for my help and then tried to blackmail me when things didn't go his way. I knew he was self-centered, but I never imagined he would pull a stunt like that.

I call my press agent. He'll have the scoop on all the publicity that's been circulating. My call goes to voice mail. Ten minutes later, Jorge knocks on my hotel door. He speaks to me in Spanish. "I got your message. And we do need to talk. The news people are having a field day with this. I brought a copy of the *Vienna Times* and a folder filled with articles I've printed from dozens of online sources."

I rub my eyes. Will this nightmare never end? "Please come in. I just made a fresh pot of coffee."

Jorge steps inside and I lead him into the dining area in the suite. He hands me a copy of the *Vienna Times* before taking a seat. Photos of me, my father, and Jade stare at me from the front page. I glance at the text and notice my mother's name is mentioned.

I swear out loud and rub my forehead.

"Just take a deep breath. Most famous people find themselves under attack at some point in their careers. We'll figure out a way to get through this," says Jorge.

I set the paper down on the table. "I'll take a closer look in a minute. Let me get our coffee."

I prepare Jorge's coffee the way he likes it with cream and *mucho azúcar*. After I serve him his coffee, I fill another cup for me and join him at the table.

"I know this will be difficult. But you need to read as much of this as you can tolerate." He pushes the thick folder toward me. I look at the local paper first. I read, teeth clenched, how my father grew tired of my mother's endless affairs. I read on.

"She knew how to manipulate men," Stefano Esperanza said to a team of reporters following the Vienna concert. Luca learned how to use women the same way his mother used men, Mr. Esperanza declared. "That's why he always bounces from one relationship to another. That Jade will end up just like the others."

What starts as an ache in my chest transforms to a stabbing pain. I could never have prepared myself for this. It was awful enough that my father left all of us alone and vulnerable, when my brothers and my sister were just kids.

But now he has the nerve to come back to ask me for favors and when he didn't get what he wants, he made it his mission to destroy everything I've worked hard for.

I read the rest of this article and then open the folder and thumb through the articles Jorge has printed out. One or two news articles question my father's motivations in trashing my reputation, but most of them lean in his favor. I close the folder and gaze up at Jorge. More than thirty minutes have passed and neither of us has said a word.

"Please, Jorge, you have to listen to me. This is nothing but lies. My mother was faithful. She sacrificed everything for us. I have had many relationships. That's never been a secret. But Jade isn't like all those women. I love Jade. I love her so much. Even though she ran away after all this happened. I need you to believe me. I need you to stand up for me and for my mother if the reporters won't listen to me. I need you to help me. To help all of us. Lorenzo, Raphael, Steve and Larry—all their careers are at stake here."

Jorge looks at me with large, sad eyes. "I've known you for a long time, Luca. And I believe you. I don't know if there's any way to turn this around. But I'm damn well going to do everything in my power to try."

"Maybe it would be better for you to walk away while you can. I don't want to ruin everything you've worked hard for, Jorge."

He fidgets with his beard and frowns. "No. Your fans must hear the truth. I need to know about everything that happened that night in Vienna so we can come up with a strategy."

"I understand. What would you like to know?"

"Tell me about the conversation you had with your father after I left."

I explain how my father wanted to use my image to launch his own business, then turned around and threatened me when I refused.

Jorge frowns and one dark brow lifts, wrinkling his forehead. "Why didn't you do it? You had a chance to save yourself."

"At the cost of everything I believe in. My career and my life would become meaningless the day I allowed a man like my father to manipulate me. I could never support him. He spewed out the most terrible lies about my mother. He spoke to Jade like she was dirt he'd scraped off his shoe. He's an evil man and the world needs to know that as the truth."

Jorge reaches out and squeezes my arm. "I'm with you on this." He pauses for a moment, tapping the side of his coffee cup with his finger. "Okay, here's what I think we should do. We should cancel the rest of the tour. People have been contacting the ticket offices, asking for refunds. I'll contact the news outlets and try to get you some interviews. You need to have opportunities to tell your side of the story."

I sit up straighter in my seat. "That sounds like a good plan, Jorge. I'll speak to anyone willing to hear what I have to say. And I want everyone who purchased a ticket—whether they ask for a refund or not—to get their money back."

"I will make some calls."

"Thank you, Jorge. Thanks for having my back on this."

Jorge smiles. "That's why you pay me the big bucks." A hint of emotion is apparent his voice. "You're a good man, Luca. I'll help you win this fight." After he stands up, I accompany him toward the door.

We share a manly hug. "Thank you, Jorge. I appreciate everything you're trying to do. We'll get through this," I say, sounding much more confident than I feel.

Once Jorge leaves, I sip my coffee and pace around the room. I suddenly think of mamá. I should have called her sooner. If she reads all of these headlines without hearing from me, she'll be devastated. I know my father's lies about her won't bother her a bit. She's used to those. But I know how upset she will be when she hears that my father's words are bringing down my career. The pain of the thought twists in my gut. For her sake and for the sake of my guys, I have to do whatever it takes to save my career. I pick up my cell phone and call her.

CHAPTER THIRTY-THREE

Jade

The first morning I'm home in San Carlos, I rush down to the sea to swim. I propel myself through the water as fast as I can, attempting to drown my despair in the sea. My tears fill up my goggles, salty like the sea. I feel empty, broken. No one will ever love me, I tell myself. As I continue to swim, the pain starts to ease. I taste the salt on my lips. Feel the gentle lift of the waves. Watch my fingers pulling through the blue-green water.

I spot three dolphins in front of me. They dive down and glide underneath me. I recognize one of them as Nick. I hear their clicks and squeaks. "It's good to see you, again," I say through the water. It has been too long since I've been out here in the sea, in this one place where I feel safe. I missed the water so much and now I'm finally here and it feels amazing.

I don't have to feel defeated. Being alone won't be that bad. I'll heal day by day in the sea. I feel a tug of pain in my heart. I miss Luca. He's thousands of miles away and I'll never see him again. And I could never settle for another man after being with Luca. He was everything I ever wanted in a man and much more. But I made my decision and there's no turning back.

He must know we weren't right for each other. He must know that I need a quiet life and am not the right woman to stand beside him in the limelight. I keep telling myself this over and over. And in some ways it makes sense. In others I feel like I took the easy way out. At the first signs of difficulty I ran. That's not what a committed partner does in a relationship.

The more I think about it, the more I realize I have more strength than I give myself credit for. I grew up with almost no emotional support from my family, but still excelled in school and as a competitive swimmer. I've been financially independent all of my adult life. And after Brandon left me, I moved to another country, adapted to all the changes, and rebuilt my life.

That's not the me who abandoned the man I loved at the first sign of hardship. But it doesn't change the fact that I did abandon him, that I did run away. Even if it's unrealistic, I wish things had turned out differently. Every fiber of my being misses him. The man, not the celebrity. I keep seeing his brilliant blue-green eyes, hearing his deep gentle voice, imagining his sometimes tender, sometimes fiery touch.

I hear a dolphin sound under the water. A sorrowful cry. Nick swims underneath me again, turning on his side to make eye contact. He seems to have something to say. The sad sound echoes below me again. Somehow, Nick senses my suffering. He knows how sad and empty I feel without Luca by my side.

CHAPTER THIRTY-FOUR

Jade

Two days after I get home, my cell phone rings. My hair's still wet. I just walked in the door from a swim. I glance at the caller ID and grimace. It's my sister, Kelsi. Shit. I'm not in the mood to talk to her, but I know she'll keep calling until I pick up. I dry my ear with my towel before answering.

"Hi, Kels—"

"Where have you been? I've been trying to call you f—"

"I was on an international fl—"

"I'm coming down there to see you. We have a lot to talk about."

"You're coming down here? When?"

"Right now. I'm topping off my car with gas at the border. I should be there by dinner time."

I rub my head. No. This can't be happening. I can't deal with Kelsi. Not now. "Wait, Kelsi, this really isn't a good time."

When she doesn't respond, I realize she's already hung up. "Dammit." I toss the phone onto the couch. Today is no different from any other day. Once again, she didn't hear a word I said. She's only attuned to her own voice. Her wants and needs are all that matter. Tears stream down my face. I don't know what to do. I pace around my living room, wringing my hands. I hear a knock at the door.

I open the door, prepared to unleash my frustration on whoever's outside. It's Justin. I bite my lip, wanting to scream. Could this day get any worse? "What do you want?" I ask in an irritated voice.

"Good morning to you, too." Justin's gaze travels the length of me and lingers on my face. "You look like shit today."

My hands tremble with rage. The nerve of this guy. "Thanks for the compliment. Look, I'm really not in the mood to talk."

"I guess your trip to Europe with lover boy didn't go so well. I've been reading all about it in the news." He glances at the sheets of paper he's holding.

That's what this is all about. I snatch them from his hand and slam the door in his face. Why can't this guy just leave me alone?

I carry the wrinkled pages back inside and sink down into a chair. I thumb through them, studying the photos of Luca, of me, of his father. It includes all of the accusations I heard that night and much more. How Luca's father left because of his mother's infidelity, how Luca has never stayed with the same woman for long. I am described as "just another sleazy groupie." One article mentions that Luca has canceled the rest of his Europe tour.

This proves that Luca isn't what he seemed, says a quote from a former fan, who added she wouldn't be attending any more of Luca's concerts. I wonder if the media ever gave Luca a chance to defend himself or whether they were more interested in hearing all the juicy lies.

Only two people spoke in his defense. His press agent, Jorge, said "Luca is a man of integrity. His words can be trusted. He asked me to fight to defend his mother's honor. He's devastated by his father's attempts to slander her. He wants his fans to know that his mother provided love and support for him and his brothers and sister when his father abandoned the family. Luca hadn't seen his father since he was a boy. His father only came to the concert for one reason—to blackmail Luca into helping him launch his online business. When Luca refused, he made up all these lies to damage his career."

Luca's brother, Lorenzo, said, "Jade was good for my brother. She was special to him. I noticed it the first time they were together. How connected they were, how happy he seemed whenever she was with him." Tears flood my eyes. The words blur together. I blink away my tears and read on. "She was the one."

Lorenzo spoke of me in past tense. I was the one. Before I left Luca there alone to deal with his lying father and to face the paparazzi, who made it their mission to tear him to shreds. Despair tears at my heart.

How could I have been so weak? How could I have left the man I love when he needed me the most? If only I'd mentally prepared myself for the possibility of reporters hounding me, maybe I wouldn't have become crazed and panicked. Anyone facing my situation would have been intimidated. The whole thing was scary as hell. But still…I could have taken a few deep breaths, pretended they were all butt naked and told the reporters all that I've seen in Luca—that he is kind, loyal and caring. That he's proved to me that I'm more than a passing fling.

But I didn't stay to defend him. I ran. And reading about the consequences of my actions makes me feel like total shit. I never imagined that breaking another person's heart could hurt even worse than having my own heart crushed. I bury my head in my hands and sob. I've never felt so miserable in my life.

CHAPTER THIRTY-FIVE

Jade

I take a shower, tug on a sun dress and rush into the bathroom to put on makeup. I can do this, I can hold it together. I'm just going to need a lot of wine to do it. I'll make a quick trip to the store before Kelsi gets here. I'll buy what we need to eat along with *mucho vino.*

If I hurry, I'll have plenty of time to down a few glasses and numb my brain before Kelsi gets here. I have to stop feeling. To get my mind to slow down for a while. I need a break from thinking over and over again about how I blew it with Luca. And worrying about how I'm going to entertain my high maintenance sister. Hopefully, she'll hate it here and won't stay more than a day or two.

I stare at my face in the mirror. To say I look like hell is an understatement. I don't even recognize the woman I see in the mirror. She's broken. Shattered. Overwhelmed. Because her heart aches to be with the love of her life.

I smear on foundation. My washed-out pallor shows right through the layer of makeup. And I'm not going to even attempt to wear mascara. It's too risky. I keep randomly bursting into tears. People might not notice my red, swollen eyes. Or the shadows under them. But streaks of black on my cheeks would be a dead giveaway of my despair.

I have never been such a mess. Not even after Brandon left me. It was his choice to dump me. There was nothing I could do to change that. But this relationship with Luca was different. He wanted to be with me. And we were right for each other in many ways. Luca made me feel grounded and comfortable with myself, much like the sea makes me feel during a swim.

Being with Luca made me realize how wrong Brandon and I were for each other all along. Then I walked—no, ran away—abandoning the man I love when he needed me most. And now I'm past tense, out of his life. I was the one but not any longer because of the choice I made out of fear. Somehow, I have to find a way to live with that.

Two hours later, I'm sitting out on my patio, refilling my glass of wine. I look out at the blue-green sea, noticing how it disappears on the horizon. What if I just swam out there as far as I could go? It's seventy or more miles to the other side of the Sea of Cortez. How long would I last in the deepest part of the sea before a shark took me out or one of those giant squids attacked. Apparently, they attack fisherman on a regular basis. They attack in groups, pummeling a person in the chest. And once the person is stunned, they use their tentacles to pull him or her in closer where their beak grinds the person up for consumption.

Yes, that's just what I need to be thinking about to boost my mood: being attacked by murderous squids. I should be thinking of a logical way to get my act together. I was starting to feel better until I saw the news headlines and Kelsi announced her impending arrival. It's all too much. Especially, my sister's visit. I don't know how I'm going to deal with that now.

I stagger to the door when I hear the knock. I open it and see my sister standing there. As usual, her hair and makeup are flawless. She's wearing jeans and gold heels and a sleeveless pale blue blouse. An enormous suitcase is sitting downstairs on the walkway. "Hi, Kelsi. You're looking great as always. Come on in."

"Hi, Jade."

I hug her. She wraps her hand around my back in a limp, unenthusiastic way and then steps back.

"Tell me what you've been up to. And how's Mia?"

"Can you bring my suitcase in for me? It's really heavy. And I already had to drag it a mile down the sidewalk."

"Oh, yeah, sure. Come on in and make yourself comfortable while I go get it." I step outside, walk down the stairs and heave the suitcase up one stair at a time, feeling an uncomfortable wrench in my shoulder. What the hell did she pack in here? Boulders?

Eventually I manage to roll the suitcase inside. I know from experience that a joke about how heavy it is wouldn't go over well with her at all. It would only lead her to say something sarcastic about what I'd take on a trip—like I'd probably only take a back pack, since I only wear swimsuits and gym clothes. "I'll put this in your room. Do you want to see it?"

She fans her face with her hand. "Not now. Just get me a drink."

I turn away, and push the suitcase down the hall to the guest room. When I return, I put some ice in a glass and fill it using water from my reverse osmosis filter.

She wrinkles her nose when I hand the glass to her. "You expect me to drink water from the tap in Mexico? Are you trying to kill me?"

The thought didn't cross my mind until now. But having to deal with her self-centered ways when I'm barely holding it together is almost too much. Right now, pushing her off the balcony sounds like an excellent idea. "Kelsi, it's been filtered with reverse osmosis."

"Whatever. I'm still not drinking any water here unless it's from a bottle."

I take the glass from her and pour the water into the sink. "Okay, fine. I've got some bottled water I keep in case of hurricanes. But it's not cold." I leave the room and grab a bottle from the back of my walk-in closet.

I pour her a glass of the warm water and hand it to her. Then I pour myself another glass of wine and take a long swallow. "How was your trip?"

"Awful. There's so much traffic in Hermosillo. And this place is ugly. Everything's random and disorderly. I don't know how you can live down here. Haven't you had enough? Don't you want to go back to America where you can live a decent life?"

Ugly? I don't think so. Maybe there are unfinished buildings here and there and every house doesn't look exactly like the one next to it, but there's something comforting about Mexico's uniqueness and disorder. What I really love is how people are warm and friendly and how life moves slower. And, of course, there is the beautiful sea. "I'm happy here, Kelsi. Did you come all this way to try to persuade me to leave? Why can't you just accept that what's good for me might be different from what you want?"

"I didn't come down here for that reason. You're the only one who can help me with my little problem."

Here it comes. "What problem?"

She raises her free hand and studies her red-painted fingernails. "We've been together now since before you left. But some issues have come up and I'm not sure how to deal with them."

"Wait, back up. You've been together? With who?"

She sighs and rolls her eyes. "With Brandon, of course. He told me when he broke up with you, he told you about us."

Prickly heat scratches at my skin and my chest feels like creatures inside are fighting to get out. My body starts to shake. Kelsi didn't just say what I think she said, did she? I leap from my chair, spilling wine down my front. "What the fuck?" I take a step toward her.

She cringes in her chair, her eyes wide with what looks like surprise mixed with fear. "Uh, I..."

I lean toward her and shake my finger in the air. "You're the one Brandon left me for?"

"Yes. He said he told you." She pushes my hand away from her face and frowns. "It was months ago, you must be over it by now. Anyway, since you were with him for a while I thought maybe you could give me some advice. He's not very adventurous in bed and I can't seem to persuade him to try anything."

I'm too stunned to cut her off mid-sentence or slap her, which would have been my normal reaction to this insanity. Instead, I stand in front of her, my mouth open like a beached fish gasping for breath, thinking WTF? But when it hits me what she's just said, I burst out laughing. This situation is absurd. "Let me get this straight. You stole my boyfriend and now that your sex life isn't working out so well, you want me to give you advice?" I clap my hands together and laugh again. "This really is classic. And another perfect example of why I left the States."

She jumps out of her chair and pushes her way around me. She must see my retracted fist. "You have to be over him by now."

I grab her blouse near the neckline and jerk, tearing the fabric. "Why is it you always think you're the expert on me? Oh, I know, it's because you're so self-absorbed, you think what you think and feel is all that matters and that everyone else should see the world from your distorted point of v—"

Kelsi takes a step back, stumbling as one of her heels catches in a tile grout line. "Now, wait."

"Let me give you some advice. And this time you better tune in for once in your life. You have two minutes to grab your suitcase and get the hell out of here. I'm not going to carry it down the stairs for you. You can carry all that heavy crap yourself. If you're not out of my condo in two minutes, I'm going to call security and you can find out what it's like to spend a night in a Mexican jail. Spoiler alert: you might want to avoid that experience if at all possible."

Her eyes widen with shock and there's a tremor in her voice. I'll be damned. She is actually listening for once. "Wait, Jade, we can work this out."

I give her shoulder a shove. "No, Kelsi, we can't. Just… go."

"Please. Won't you just help me with my suitcase?"

I burst out laughing again. "You really don't get it, do you? I'm done with you, Kelsi. I don't ever want to speak to you again."

She slinks into the guest bedroom, retrieves her suitcase, and quietly leaves my condo. I stare out the window and finish the rest of my wine. Then I pull on a swimsuit.

CHAPTER THIRTY-SIX

Jade

I'm trembling as I weave my way down to the beach. I've had way too much wine, or maybe not nearly enough. My view of the sea and the surrounding mountains, shadowed by the late afternoon sun, shifts and sways. I hiccup once, then again, tasting the bitter flavor of partially digested wine. I know it's unwise to swim intoxicated, but right now I don't care. I'm too upset. This day has been a total nightmare and the sea's my only chance for calming down.

Just when I thought my life couldn't get any worse…Kelsi calls. As if it weren't bad enough that I had to even see her when I'm falling apart, the reason she came made it ten times worse. I can't believe she stole my boyfriend from me. It makes me feel like total shit.

It's like a confirmation of what my parents always said. Kelsi has it. I don't. But I think they were wrong. Kelsi is a selfish bitch. I've never been like that. I've always been a good listener. I've always been honest. I've always been dependable. At least until recently, I think when Luca's face flashes in front of my eyes.

I dive into the water and start swimming furiously. The bitter mingling of old wine mixed with saltwater leaves me with the worst taste in my mouth I've ever experienced. Blech. I burp again when I breath. Apparently, wine and swimming don't mix. Once I establish a rhythm, I start to enjoy the freedom of swimming, unconstrained by my safety buoy. I know it's dangerous. But it's only one time.

I stroke harder, faster. Tears flow from my eyes, filling my goggles as my mind drifts back to Luca. I see the soft lines that appeared around his eyes and mouth whenever he smiled. How flashes of light appeared in his blue-green eyes sometimes when he looked at me, the way the sunlight dances like brilliant diamonds across the sea.

God, how I miss him. Luca proved to me that he cared. I know he loved me. I was enough for him. I was. Until I deserted him.

I kick harder and take long, frantic pulls through the water. I made a mistake. I shouldn't have left him. I should have stood up to those reporters and told them every amazing thing I know about Luca. I shouldn't have been thinking that if Brandon left me, Luca might also. Hearing what happened from my sister confirms how shallow Brandon really was. In order to have someone beautiful on the outside, he's willing to settle for a woman who's a self-centered bitch on the inside. Luca would never do that. He doesn't expect me to lose weight or wear anything fancy or do anything other than be myself.

Luca and I may have been born in two different countries, but in many way's we're similar. We both value honesty and artistic expression and thrive being in quiet places where we can connect with nature.

I'm not going to let my defeatist thoughts ruin my only chance of lasting happiness. I'm going to contact every media outlet I can track down. I'm going to talk to the reporters and tell them the truth. And then I have to beg Luca to forgive me.

I hear the whine of a motor. A boat or a jet ski? I wonder if it sees me. I breathe to the front to check and feel a sudden splitting pain in my head. And then there's only blackness.

CHAPTER THIRTY-SEVEN

Luca

I sit alone outside on my eighth-floor balcony looking over the water. I rented a condo on Algodones Beach in San Carlos, about as far away from Jade as I can get. I swallow the rest of my beer, setting the empty bottle down. I stand up to grab another one when my cell phone rings.

I glance at the caller ID. What does Jorge want? Probably confirmation as to whether I want to go on tour next week. I haven't decided yet one way or another. After the media frenzy I've endured, I'm not sure it's worth it. My father won. He didn't get his way, so he ruined my reputation. And he took my mother's down with mine. The bastard. I swallow the rest of the bottle of beer and set the empty bottle down with a crash on the table. Then I grab the phone and say, "*Buenas tardes.*"

"Are you drinking again?" Jorge asks.

"Maybe. What do you want?" I speak more rudely than I intended. But lately, I've been feeling impatient and angry all the time.

"Have you heard about Jade?"

A muscle tightens in my chest. "What about her?"

"A boat hit her while she was out swimming. She's in the Hospital San José in Hermosillo."

Suddenly, Jade's abandonment doesn't matter. All that matters now is her well-being. I want to run to her. I want to be there for her. If she wants me. "*Dios mío, no.* Is she going to be okay?"

"I'm not sure. The doctors say she lost a lot of blood and suffered a concussion."

"Oh, no. This is terrible. How did you hear about it?"

"After the accident and in the hospital, she kept asking for you. It's all over the news. I called you the minute I heard the report."

I feel another piercing pain in my heart. My dear Jade is in the hospital fighting for her life. I was the one she thought of during her darkest hour. I have to get to her. I have to know she is okay. I can't lose her. Not like this. "I'm on my way to the hospital."

CHAPTER THIRTY-EIGHT

Jade

I awaken, feeling groggy. But that's the least of my worries. My head feels like a cracked egg. It hurts like hell. I instinctively reach for my face before I try to open my eyes. My head is sheathed in thick bandages. Touching my forehead sends a jolt of pain knifing through me. What happened? I open my eyes to see I'm in a hospital room. I hear the beep of my heart monitor. Outside the room, I hear people speaking in Spanish.

All my memories come tumbling back. The many glasses of wine. Kelsi's arrival. Her devastating news. My swim in the sea. The sound of the boat motor. Sudden pain.

The *panga* must have struck me. It was idiotic of me to swim without my safety buoy. I'm lucky I'm not dead. I remember how I was thinking of Luca when something hit me. I'm still not sure if it was a boat or a jet ski.

I wish more than anything Luca were here with me now. He would sit beside the bed and talk to me in his sexy, soothing voice. Just having him near would make the pain in my head bearable. I wouldn't even be in this damn hospital if I hadn't left him.

Oh, why did I make such a terrible mistake? All my fear and doubt made any chance of a future for the two of us completely impossible.

But out there in the water, everything became crystal clear. I knew then, and I know now that I'm strong enough to face the media, to stand up for the man I love even if he doesn't want me anymore. Luca's career is in trouble and even if there's no future for us, I want to do everything I can to try to turn things around for him.

A nurse with dark hair piled into a bun on top of her head rushes into the room. *"It's good to see that you're awake,"* she says in Spanish. *"Me llamo Marisol."* She's wearing thick makeup and purple-tinted lipstick.

"Con mucho gusto," I manage.

Marisol's forehead crinkles in worry. *"Señorita, I need to move you to another room right away. But we must wait for another nurse to arrive to help me."*

"Why are you moving me?"

"There are many reporters downstairs. They are saying you had a romantic relationship with Luca Espinoza. They know what room you're in."

Another nurse rolls a mobile bed into the room and asks her if she's *lista.*

This is the opportunity I've been waiting for, my chance to make things right again. *"No, wait. I want to talk to them. I should have talked to them when I was in Vienna. I need to clear up all of this misinformation for Luca's sake."*

The two women look at each other for a moment and shake their heads. *"It will be too stressful for you, dear."*

"Por favor. Es muy, muy importante."

"Muy bien," she says. *"But only for a few minutes. Then I'm going to make them leave so you can rest."*

"Está bien."

I hear running footsteps on the tile floor before the four reporters enter the room. Marisol holds up a hand, speaking to them sternly. She tells them I have a concussion, that they need to stay a few feet back from the bed and can only stay for *pocos minutos*.

A female reporter wearing a navy-blue business suit steps slowly toward the bed. She's young, her smooth skin covered in a thick layer of makeup, her lips bright red with lipstick. She introduces herself to me as Alicia and tells me she's with *Mexico News Daily*. After introducing me to the other reporters in the room, she turns back toward me. "*Please tell me about your accident*?" she asks in Spanish.

I use the remote to raise my head so I can meet Alicia's gaze. Thankfully, some of the throbbing pain in my head subsides. "*I was swimming in the sea when a fishing boat struck me.*"

"*Is it true that Luca Espinoza was your boyfriend?*"

My heart skips a beat hearing our relationship mentioned in the past tense. I wish more than anything it was just beginning instead of already over. I think of that first night he kissed me. And how I thought about that kiss almost every minute of every day until I saw him again. "*Sí. Es verdad.*"

"*Did you leave him because of another woman?*" asks the male reporter with a moustache named Juan.

"*No, there was no other woman.*"

"*Then why did you leave?*" Alicia asks.

"*Because I was afraid. I—*"

"*Afraid of what?*" Juan asks.

"*Please let me finish. This is important, and I don't want to be interrupted.*"

"*Please go ahead,*" says Alicia. She side-eyes the men with her to shut them up.

"Is it okay if I say it in English?"

"*Sí, por supuesto,*" says Alicia. The others nod.

"For eight years, I stayed in a relationship with a man I couldn't trust and who didn't even know who I really was. Maybe I put up with him because I never liked myself all that much. My parents criticized me until the day they died in a plane crash. My sister slept with my now ex-boyfriend while we were still together. I came to Mexico to escape all the negativity that was holding me down. I started swimming in the sea every day, which has a been a wonderful experience—at least, until recently. I met a wonderful couple—Gabriela and Martin—who treat me like family. They're on their way here now to see me. And then I met Luca. And I knew right away he was special."

"Where did you meet?" Alicia asks.

"On a beach in San Carlos. I had been out swimming and when I came to shore we started talking and he asked me if I could give him a swimming lesson."

Alicia and the others laugh. "Now that's a pick-up line I haven't heard before."

"I know, right? That's what I thought at first when he asked me to teach him—that Luca was just looking for a reason to see me again. And that was true, but he genuinely wanted to learn. He saw me out there swimming with the dolphins and wanted to know what it was like. I worked with him, he made the effort to learn, and I was able to take him out in the water to see those amazing creatures close up. We've had so much fun together. Luca and I had a special connection. And he encouraged me to stop being hard on myself.

But it's hard to change old patterns of thinking. I'd gotten used to thinking of myself as not good enough, of being unworthy. Then when his father showed up in Vienna and made up all those lies about him and his mother, I ran away because I was afraid to face all those reporters. I was afraid they would expose all of my vulnerabilities and that I would be an embarrassment to Luca.

I realize now that I was only thinking of myself. I didn't consider that my leaving would lead reporters to conclude his father's words were the truth. I love Luca and I should have been the loudest voice, the first person stepping up to defend him. I left then, but now I want you to know that Luca deserves better than everything I've been reading online everywhere. His father's a liar and an evil man. Luca is not only a talented artist, he's kind and compassionate and fun to be around. That's why I fell in love with him. He's honest—no one should doubt his word."

My voice thickens with emotion. "I wish I could say this to Luca now. I know it's too late to save what we had after all the mistakes I've made." Tears stream down my face. I wipe them away with the hand not attached to an IV. "I want him to know that I will always remember our time together and I'll never forget how special he made me feel. And I will always love him."

Alicia dabs her mascara-enhanced eyes with a tissue. "Oh, *señorita,* that is the most romantic story I've ever heard. Thank you for sharing your story with me. But perhaps it is time for you to tell Luca this in person. Because he is here. Now."

CHAPTER THIRTY-NINE

Jade

My gaze snaps toward the door. The heart monitor suddenly starts beeping very fast. I jerk up straight in the hospital bed, tugging the IV line too tight. A pulse of sudden pain in my head makes the room spin. I don't care. He's here. Luca really is here.

"Jade," Luca says as he rushes into the room. He speaks in a firm, but polite voice to the reporters in Spanish. *"Please leave us. There's been too much excitement already. She needs to rest."*

"I want to ask you a few questions," says the male reporter with the moustache.

"Más tarde," he says. Later.

The female reporter reprimands the male reporter and makes a move to push him out.

"Muy bien," he says. The reporters quickly shuffle out of the room.

Luca's by my bed in an instant, taking hold of my hand and warming my cold fingers with his strong, calloused hands.

"I'm sorry, Luca. I made a mistake. I was afraid, I wasn't thinking straight."

He strokes my cheek with his fingers. He's so gentle, careful, making sure his fingers don't touch the battered parts of my head and face. "You don't have to apologize. I understand."

"I wasn't prepared for all those reporters. But I shouldn't have panicked. Ever since I left, I kept thinking back and wishing I could do it all over again."

"I know that, Jade. But it doesn't matter anymore. We're together again. Please, you must stop worrying. You've been in an accident. What you need now is rest, Jade." The gentle way he says my name feels like a caress. He kisses my cheek softly.

His warm lips on my face are such a comfort. Having him near, smelling his man scent—make me feel infinitely better. It was scary being alone in this hospital, but now that he's with me, I feel safe again, like everything is going to be all right.

"Thank you for coming here. I missed you so much, Luca."

"Why were you swimming without your swim buoy?"

"Oh, Luca, it was terrible. I've been such a wreck since I got back, but I was trying to hold it together." The words tumble from my lips and I tell him about Justin bringing by the news articles and my sister showing up uninvited and her shocking news. "It was just too much. I already started drinking when I knew she was coming and after I made her leave, I fell apart. I shouldn't have gone swimming in the first place, but I thought it would be the only way to get back my equilibrium."

Luca's face turns a shade darker and his heavy brows merge in anger. "Oh, Jade. I wish I had been there to protect you."

"It's over now."

"*Gracias a Dios* you're okay. When my press agent said you were in the hospital, I rushed to get here."

"Even after what I did?"

"I understand why you were afraid, Jade. You know how I feel about being pursued by the paparazzi. It can be a nightmare. I'll make sure that you never have to talk to any reporters unless you want to."

"I love you, Luca. More than anything."

He kisses me softly on the lips. "I love you, too," he whispers.

CHAPTER FORTY

Two months later

Luca

For more than a month, I've been living with Jade in her San Carlos condominium whenever I'm not on tour. I wake up beside her, my hands still wrapped around her waist, the front of my body molded to the back of hers. Our bodies fit perfectly together. It's comforting to nestle in close to her soft, smooth skin. I bury my nose in the coconut and citrus scent of her hair. Being near her when I awaken instantly arouses me. I want her. I shift her hair over enough that I can kiss the nape of her neck and the soft skin on the back of her shoulder. She stirs and rolls over to face me. "*Buenos días.*" Her sleepy eyes gaze up at me, large and bright.

"*Buenos días, mi amor.*" Jade is the love of my life. Being with her makes me feel complete.

Golden heat flashes in her dark eyes. Her instant response amps my heat level up another notch. Is it my Spanish words or my erection that excite her? She told me once my accent and speaking Spanish turn her on. Ever since, I've been speaking *mucho español* when we're in bed. Anything to make the experience as mind blowing as possible for her. Giving her pleasure thrills me.

Everything about Jade excites me—her dark, flirtatious eyes, her full breasts, her athletic body—especially her legs that have been sculpted into sheer perfection from so many kilometers of swimming. She's an incredible swimmer. Last week she won her age category in the 1800-meter, *Cruce de Bahía Miramar* sea swimming race that took place near here. I was there to see her standing up on top of the podium to receive her gold medal.

Right now, I ache to have Jade's strong legs wrapped around my waist, I ache to sink deep inside her wet warmth.

I press my lips against hers and she grips the back of my head to pull me in closer. Our mouths collide in a crushing kiss. I slide my tongue over the crevice of her lips, begging for entry. She opens to me and our tongues meet and mingle, exploring, tantalizing.

The smoldering desire I feel for her bursts into flame. I'm desperate to take possession of her. Jade belongs to me. She's mine today and forever. Now we can meet skin to skin with no condoms between us. Jade's taking birth control and we've had blood tests to prove our clean health.

I kiss one of her breasts and she shivers and releases a ragged breath. My cock twitches again. I love to make her feel good. Her sighs and moans of pleasure turn me on. I flick my tongue over one nipple until it hardens in my mouth. I work my tongue around her whole breast, savoring its full shape and softness. She tosses her head and then lets it fall back on the pillow, splaying her beautiful dark hair in every direction as she groans with pleasure. "Oh, Luca, this feels so good."

"Being with you feels so good. All of it."

She smiles and gazes at me with heavy-lidded eyes. "Yes. It does."

I capture her other breast with my mouth while my hand skims over the swell of her hips and across her abdomen until it meets the juncture between her thighs. My fingers meet a wet gush of her arousal. "*You're so wet, Jade,*" I say in Spanish.

"I want you Luca." Her voice is ragged with lust.

Sometimes, I make love to her slowly. When I sense her desire is too intense, I possess her right away to take the edge off. After she comes the first time, then I can skim my lips over every inch of her body or make love to her five different ways.

I open her legs wider with one knee before straddling her hips. I spread her nether lips open with my finger, feeling a painful ache in my cock as I see how slick and wet she is.

I line the head of my cock up at the entrance of her opening. Jade bites her lip and grinds her hips up toward me. I smile with satisfaction seeing how greedy she is for me to take her. It's so hot. I sink in inch by inch, grimacing as the wanton sensation of her walls contracting around my cock seizes me. I have to use every ounce of will to maintain control. Her wet walls squeeze my sensitive cock so tightly, I twist with erotic pleasure. Damn. Being inside her feels so good. I could easily lose all control and come too soon. But I won't. Her pleasure matters the most. Watching her fall apart makes me crazy. I bury myself to the hilt inside her, gritting my teeth as more hot sensation grips me. "*Dios te sientes bien. Eres tan hermosa.* (God, you feel good. You're so beautiful)."

She bucks up against me and my rhythm intensifies. Her skin glistens with sweat. The wet slap of our bodies is such a turn on. Jade moans again, making the most animalistic sounds a human can make. I'm panting and out of breath, equally crazed with lust. I ram my cock deep inside her again.

"Oh, yes, Luca," Jade groans. "Fuck me harder." She writhes beneath me, her face contorted with ecstasy. Her moans and pants grow more urgent. I know she's teetering on the edge of orgasm. I continue to thrust into her, watching her thrash and scream as she shatters. Her walls squeeze tighter and her orgasm drenches my cock. I continue to thrust inside her, wringing spasm after spasm from her body. Once her climax ends, I allow the white-hot pleasure to consume me. I thrust in deep and pause. And then I explode, my seed shooting deep inside her.

After two more hours of sweaty lovemaking and breakfast, we're walking hand in hand toward the beach. Our free hands hold swimming equipment. Most mornings, we swim together. Everything's better than ever with my career. People no longer believe my father's lies. He recently got arrested for assaulting a reporter.

My new album—Swimming with Dolphins—featuring the single *Jade's Song* is at the top of the charts in the US, Mexico, Australia, and Italy.

The interviews I'd planned to set up to promote Jade's books didn't turn out to be necessary. She became a sensation almost overnight, hitting the *USA Today* and *New York Times* bestseller lists with her latest release, *Forever by the Sea*. Reading the erotic scenes in Jade's novel made me desperate to make love to her. Afterward, I scooped her up and took her straight to the bedroom. All the books in her backlist are becoming popular, too. I knew she had talent and that if more people discovered her books, she'd become a big success.

"Which way do you want to swim today?" Jade asks.

"Toward the estuary."

"That works for me." Her whole face lights up when she smiles. Even her eyes have a special sparkle. I still remember how much her smile thrilled me the first time I saw her here. She made me feel special right from the start. I love her more than I ever imagined I could love any woman. She's not only beautiful, she's smart and creative and kind.

We wade out in the water, shuffling our feet. Then we swim ten or so meters out and start swimming parallel to shore. I'll never be as strong of a swimmer as she is, but wearing fins, I can almost keep up with her. She swims beside me most mornings to match my slower tempo. Once my Garmin shows that I've done 750 meters, we reverse directions and after I exit the water to start my run, Jade swims for another 30 minutes or more.

Most days, we see the dolphins. We heard later from the fisherman captaining the boat that hit Jade that two dolphins had been frantically jumping and slapping the water with their tails shortly before the accident happened. One even swam right in front of the boat just before it struck her, making it slow its speed. The dolphins hadn't been able to prevent the accident, but by getting the boat to slow down, they may have saved her life.

Tonight, I'll ask Jade to marry me. The platinum engagement ring I had custom designed for her has a large heart-shaped solitaire diamond with two small platinum dolphins on either side of it. I can't wait to slip that ring on her finger. To hear her say that she'll be mine. Forever.

"Look," Jade says, pointing in front of us. She starts swimming a slow breaststroke. They must be near us. I raise my head forward on my next breath to take a look.

Three dolphins arc up over the water and dive down in front of us. Seconds later, I see their long sleek white and gray bodies pass underneath us. Their large size doesn't intimidate me anymore. They're *amigos*. They don't come this close to me too often. But it's a special experience whenever they do. They surround Jade whenever she's alone out in the water. It's almost as though when I'm not with her, they stay near her to keep her safe.

Two dolphins swim underneath us again. They're so close, I can hear their clicking sounds. I never imagined I'd get this close to one of these magnificent creatures. But the first day I saw Jade out here swimming, that's what I wanted.

Now—thanks to Jade—it's finally happening. She's given me the opportunity to connect with the sea and these incredible creatures. The best part about this experience is that we're out here in the sea together—laughing and splashing around and admiring the dolphins.

I thrive on performing up on stage with our band. It's my career, and it's how I share my gift. But San Carlos is where I come back to renew my creativity. And Jade is here. My love. *Mi amor*. My world. *Mi mundo*. Whether I'm beside her or on tour far away, she's always close in my heart.

THE END

ABOUT SABRINA

Sabrina Devonshire, an avid swimmer most of her life, can usually be found near or immersed in a body of water. If she's not seeking an endorphin rush in a pool, lake or ocean, she's usually writing or practicing yoga.

Whenever she's stroking her way through the water, she's conjuring up new plot ideas or plans to travel to an exotic locale such as Belize or Greece. Her exotic romantic adventures offer a great escape - transporting readers to exotic places with hot alpha males where steamy sex and happily-ever-after romance reign! Sabrina lives with her husband in Arizona and San Carlos, Mexico.

Thank you so much for reading my work! I would greatly appreciate it if you would post a short review of *Jade's Song* on Amazon. Subscribe to my newsletter, read blog posts, blurbs and excerpts for new releases and more on my Exotic Romantic Adventures web site at www.sabrinadevonshireromances.com.

You can also follow me on Twitter (@SabrinaDevonsh1) and Facebook (www.facebook.com/SabrinaDevonshireFans).

Want to immerse yourself in more exotic romantic adventures? Below is a list of my other published books to date:

Telenovela (South of the Border 1)

Ocean Swimmer

Sophia's Boss (Office Interludes 1)

Doctor's Orders (Office Interludes 2)

Amalfi Affair (Navy SEALs of Valor 1)

Czech Mate (Navy SEALs of Valor 2)

French Kiss (Navy SEALs of Valor 3)

Greek God (Navy SEALs of Valor 4)

My Professor and the La Jolla Meteorite Craters

Dangerous Descent (Love in the Labyrinths 1)

The Unseen (Love in the Labyrinths 2)

Mai Tai Man

Seaside Seduction

Never Let You Go

Love in the Rainforest

My Greek SEAL

Christmas Collision

Made in the USA
San Bernardino, CA
07 December 2018